THE PROBLEM WITH WITCHES

The Elemental Witch Series: Book 2

TANIA HUTLEY

TRUDI JAYE

Chapter One

An awful moaning fills my ears. Pain flares at my side, and my neck feels like it's cemented to my shoulder. Panic churns along my nerve endings but I can't actually remember *why* I'm so filled with dread.

Forcing my eyes open, I blink at the arm of the lumpy couch I've been sleeping on. Why did I sleep on the couch? And why do my eyes feel like they've been dipped into a vat of salt and chlorine?

My gaze goes to the person next to me. The moaning is coming from Xander.

His large body is splayed awkwardly over the other side of the sofa, his legs tipped off the side and his face squashed against the cushions. He's making a tortuous sound, like he's in terrible pain.

"Xander!" I grab his shoulder to shake him awake.

The instant I touch him, my mind floods with darkness. A nasty voice penetrates my brain, the words like silent probing fingers clawing deep inside my head.

"Join me, Sapphira," it rasps, *"and you will have power beyond your wildest—"*

I jerk my hand back with a curse as a painful burning sensation spreads up my arm.

Just like I did in the Blood Council chambers, I see strands of magic, this time black and oily. They're coming from Xander, and they're oozing toward my shoulder.

I leap up, my heart hammering, and shake my arm out. The strands vanish and the feeling of my arm being on fire subsides. But I'm left with terrible memories spreading through my consciousness like a virus I can't stop.

A demon called Jeqabeel is inside Xander.

The Blood Council forced me to become one of them.

And I killed Uncle Ray. Oh God, I turned him inside out. I put my hands over my eyes, trying to banish the gruesome image of his blood-covered body.

Suddenly I remember our time limit, and jerk around to check the clock in the hallway. It's ten o'clock in the morning. The council gave us just forty-eight hours to find a way to get Jeqabeel out of Xander, and now seven of those hours are gone, wasted because we couldn't keep our eyes open.

We have forty-one hours left before the council turn Xander into a statue to keep the demon from escaping and killing us all.

Xander groans and opens his eyes. For a moment, they look blood red. My heart stutters. Am I seeing the demon inside him?

Then he blinks, and his eyes are back to their normal ice blue.

"Hey." He sits up and stretches with a grimace that tells me he's as stiff and sore as I am. "You don't want to know what I was dreaming." He shudders. "I've never been so glad to wake up."

"We shouldn't have slept so long."

"After the night we had, we both needed it." Xander

sounds way too calm. "Besides, you had to rest to get your magic back." He stands up, running his hands down the front of his jeans. "No pressure, but it'd be great if you could magic the demon out of me now."

"I wish it were that easy." I say the words without thinking and then wish I hadn't.

Xander's expression tightens, fear momentarily clouding his eyes.

I reach out to touch his arm, then remember the demon and snatch my hand back. Dammit, I've give just about anything to be able to hug him right now.

"Don't worry," I tell him. "I'll find a way." I have to, because if we don't, Xander gets turned to stone. That's some serious motivation.

"How hard will it be?" Xander's a smart guy, a detective used to reading people. He's not fooled by my show of optimism.

"My magic's been bound for years," I admit. "I don't know how to use it."

"But you'll try, right?"

I nod, because what choice do I have? "I'll do my best."

"Good. I trust you."

If only I trusted myself. Xander has far too much confidence in me, but I hate to argue when my magic's the only thing giving him hope.

I reach up to run my hand through my hair, and it gets stuck in the tangled bird's nest at the back of my head. My hair's hard to control at the best of times, let alone after a night sleeping on the sofa. "I'm going to wash up, and check on Ratticus." Sylvia's pet rat is in a cardboard box in the corner. I can hear his wheel squeaking as he runs inside it.

Xander nods. "I'll make coffee."

I emerge from the bathroom a short time later, freshly showered, wearing clean clothes, and with my hair secured in two long pigtails. Xander's in the kitchen with two steaming cups of coffee, and when he offers me one, I take hold of it with the relieved sigh of someone who's critically caffeine-depleted. Then I fall onto a slice of toast as though it's the last piece of food left on Earth.

While I'm devouring every crumb, he disappears upstairs to shower, and I make a second cup of coffee and more toast. I'm sitting at the kitchen table licking butter off my fingers when Xander comes back smelling fresh and clean, with his hair damp. He hasn't shaved for a while, and his jaw is dark with stubble. The rugged look suits him. My eyes catch on his lips. I remember all too well how amazing it felt when he kissed me. In fact, if he didn't have a demon inside him, I'd be tempted to run my fingers over his stubble while I test how soft his lips must feel in comparison—

"You okay?" Xander frowns, rubbing one hand over his bristled jaw. "Why are you staring at me like that? Do I have something on my face?"

"No." I let out a long sigh. "It's nothing. Wishful thinking, that's all."

"Are you ready to try magicking the monster out of me?"

"I'd like to." With another sigh, I pull my mind away from Xander's lips, back to the far more important question of how to save his life. "But I don't know how."

"Just zap it." He aims a stage magician's hand motion at me, as though he's shooting lightning into me from his fingertips. "Slam it with your magic."

"That's way too dangerous. Remember how I accidentally turned Agnes into a chicken? What if I do something even worse to you?"

"Worse than having a demon inside me? Worse than your council turning me into a statue?" He raises his eyebrows. "They only gave us forty-eight hours, remember. It's worth taking a risk."

I suck in a breath, thinking hard. "When I was younger, I learned spells to direct my earth magic. But I haven't used spells in a long time and Magnus said I couldn't use them to control two types of magic. Anyway, what kind of spell would banish a demon?"

He sits down next to me at the kitchen table. "Maybe there's a demon-banishing spell in the book the Unseen wanted."

"The dark magic grimoire?" It's a good idea, and he's probably right. It's far more likely than an ordinary grimoire to have spells relating to demons, especially given that it was written by the witch who brought Jeqabeel into this dimension in the first place.

It's just a shame I can't read it.

"Using dark magic is strictly forbidden," I tell him. "Besides, I left the grimoire in the library by mistake. Seeing as we almost destroyed the building, getting it back might be difficult."

"So how are we going to get the demon out of me?"

I hate having to admit I'm totally clueless. "I'm not sure." I mumble the words into my coffee cup.

"Then we'll have to try zapping it." He lifts both hands as though my magic's a football I'm aiming to throw at him, and he's ready to catch it. "Hit me with a spell."

I let out a long, reluctant breath. "Tell you what. Let me try using a spell on something other than you. Something inanimate. If I manage not to blow it up, that'll be a good start."

"Here, magic this cup." He pushes his empty coffee cup toward me. "Turn it into a chicken."

"It doesn't work like that. Give me a minute to feed Ratticus, and I'll try to remember some of the spells I used to know."

Ratticus is still running on his wheel in the cardboard box I set up for him in the living room. He climbs out of the wheel when I fill up his bowl, and I pick him up to stroke his furry back while I think.

How many earth magic spells can I recall? A few easy ones, for moving dirt and stones. And one to shape a stone into a statue. Dad taught it to me, so I could give a carving to Mom for her birthday.

Can I still remember that spell? I trace the rune in the air with the hand that's not holding Ratticus. That's it, isn't it? It's been so long, I'm not entirely sure.

"Pity you're only a rat," I tell Ratticus. "You must have watched Sylvia use dozens of spells. I bet you know lots of runes, don't you?"

"Does he ever talk back?" Xander's voice comes from close behind me. "Is Ratticus just a regular rat, or can he speak?"

I snort. "A talking rat? That's ridiculous."

"Is it? I've seen stranger things lately."

I guess he has a point.

"It'd be great if Ratticus could share Sylvia's secrets," I say wistfully. "She was an archivist, so she could use her books to do a little of every kind of magic. Unfortunately, Ratticus would need a brain a little bigger than his pea-sized one to be able to tell us anything."

I give the rat one last pat, then head back to the kitchen and pull a sharp paring knife from the drawer. I have to figure out what I'm going to do with each of my two types of magic. "Let's go outside. I'll use my earth magic on the stones in the courtyard seeing as they're already messed up." Using my magic outside will also mean less danger of bringing the house down by mistake.

Not that I'm going to say that. Not when Xander's so hopeful my power can save him.

He leads the way out the back door, and with every step my dread grows stronger. The large courtyard pavers are already in pieces, evidence of how unpredictable my magic is. The two halves of my magical whole are tangled and chaotic, the animal magic fighting against the earth magic.

Even though I can now see the magic as I'm using it, and the strands make more sense, I'm still terrified of hurting Xander. Since the explosion that killed my mother and stuck her animal magic inside me, my power has been impossible to control. Last time I tried to destroy the demon, I accidently let Jeqabeel escape into Xander.

Hardly the solution I was aiming for.

I search the mess for a stone I can use to carve a figure, and pick up one that's a little bigger than a closed fist. That'll do.

"Stand back." I lift the stone in one hand. In the other hand, I hold the paring knife in such a way that I can rest my thumb against its blade.

The Blood Council's shared magic is now inside me along with my own. The council magic is much stronger than mine, but it's balled up and isolated, like the scary monster under the bed has gotten itself tangled in a bed sheet and all it can do is growl.

Aunt Therese warned me very clearly not to use it, that it would overwhelm me if I did. Even if she hadn't, I wouldn't be the slightest bit tempted. Their magic would probably tear me to pieces if I so much as looked at it funny.

Instead I feel for my own magic, the animal and earth

magic that's enough of a tangled mess all on its own, without adding any extra power. They're both twisting inside me, waiting for the blood that will set them free.

For the spell to work, I need to cut myself, then draw a rune, preferably with my blood. When I only had earth magic, I could control it as it came out, giving me time to cast the spell. With two types of magic, it's too difficult to control the second type while performing the spell with the first one. The magic is too fast, too eager, too messed up.

Maybe if I draw the rune quickly enough, I can cast a spell with my earth magic before my animal magic does something unpredictable?

"If the spell goes to plan, the stone in my hand will turn into a small statue of a dog," I tell Xander, who's hovering beside me.

"What kind of dog?"

"A Labrador. It's going to be sitting down."

I picture the dog I want to create. When I have the image firmly in my mind, I drag my thumb along the knife's blade.

My heart pounding, I quickly draw the rune on the stone. I concentrate on trying to push the animal magic deep inside me, holding it in while letting the earth magic filter into the stone I'm holding.

At first, it seems to work. My earth magic is being directed into the stone, and it starts to morph and change. A little bubble of hope expands in my chest. Maybe I really will be able to do this.

Then my animal magic slams against the barriers inside me. It's too strong to be contained. With the Council bindings gone, it's filling me up, expanding exponentially as it strains to be free.

When I used it at the council chambers, I managed to keep the earth strands and the animal strands from getting tangled. But whatever control I had was born of utter desperation. I don't know exactly how I did it. And now it turns out I can't replicate it.

As my earth magic expands and swells into the stone, my animal magic is dragged out with it. I manage to hold it back for a moment longer—and then it's over.

Both sides burst out of me fast and hard. The strands weave around me; my animal magic sparks with unrestrained energy while the earth magic is thick and heavy with power. The force of it sets my body alight. I have as much chance of snatching lightning bolts out of the sky as controlling this much magic.

The air leaves my lungs, and for a moment, I'm breathless. Frozen in place.

I'm in the middle of a vortex, both sides of my magic swirling around me. Any control I had was just an illusion. The earth and animal magic collide and crash against each other, creating sparks of energy that amp up the magic even further.

As I try desperately to pull at least some of the magic back in, the earth magic slams into the stone in my palm so hard it explodes in my hand. I snatch my arm back with a curse, and the remaining stone pieces drop. The magic hits the paving stones with a deafening crash, and dust billows up in a giant mushroom cloud.

Through the fog of debris, a shape rises. The dust half-blinds me, but the shape is huge. Blinking hard, I make out a giant statue of a dog that's bigger than I am. My magic has created a statue out of the tiny piece of rock I gave it, pulling up more paving stones for good measure. The statue looms over me menacingly. For a moment it feels just like when the pack of possessed dogs attacked me at my house and I accidentally enlarged a savage Rottweiler. Can this dog move? Will it attack me just like the demon-dogs?

Panic flares, and I take a lurching step backward.

My foot snags on one of the broken pavers, and I stumble. I swing my arms, trying to regain my balance, and my animal magic swirls faster around me. I land heavily on my butt and let out a cry of pain.

My last tenuous hold on my magic fractures.

The animal magic arcs toward Xander, then veers away, as if repelled by the demon. It streaks toward the house and disappears.

I feel it pouring itself into the only other living creature nearby.

Ratticus.

Frantically, I try to drag the magic away from Sylvia's poor rat, but it doesn't work. I feel it transform him, but I can't tell how.

Scrambling to my feet, I stagger toward the house, dragging in a lungful of stone dust as I go. It turns my throat into sandpaper. Coughing and hacking, I double over, desperately trying to blink dirt out of my eyes.

Behind me, Xander is coughing too. He opens the back door with one hand, grabbing my arm to tug me away from the dust.

As soon as he touches me, darkness fills my brain. Burning pain, and tendrils of dark magic snake along my skin. The repulsive voice reaches inside me, whispering in my head. *"You will have your deepest, darkest desires, Sapphira. I can bring your parents back to life—"*

Still coughing, I jerk away from Xander.

"Sorry," he rasps. "Forgot."

I stumble inside to the kitchen, and hesitate at the door to the living room. What am I going to find on the other side? Perhaps I could board up the living room and never go in there again? Then I wouldn't have to see what terrible thing my animal magic has done to poor Ratticus.

Best-case scenario, he's a paving slab. Worst case… I don't want to think about it.

Behind me, Xander doesn't realise what I've done. He pours us both a glass of water, and when he hands me the glass, I gulp mine down. It soothes my throat, though using my magic has made me feel weak and shaky.

"I take it that didn't go exactly to plan?" asks Xander.

"Not exactly." I drain the glass. "It was actually a new low for me. I caused two major disasters." I glance toward the living room where Ratticus's cage is.

"Two?"

When I put my empty water glass down, a gritty, dirty handprint is imprinted on it: a souvenir of one of the disasters. I have a sick feeling that the other disaster is going to be far worse.

Ratticus has already suffered. First he watched Sylvia being killed, then he had to relive her death when he shared the memory with me. Then we were attacked by monster dogs trying to kill us. After all that, he deserves a quiet, peaceful life.

But I have to face up to what I've done to him.

I walk into the living room, forcing myself to look at his cardboard box in the corner. Or rather, to where his cardboard box used to be. It's torn into several pieces, which are scattered across the floor, together with his food and water. His wheel lies on its side by the couch, still turning in slow circles.

But where's Ratticus?

Xander makes a strangled sound. "What the——?"

Chapter Two

I follow Xander's horrified gaze to the large stack of paint tins in the corner of the room.

Crouched behind them is a monster.

Ratticus still has the body of a rat, but now he's the size of a dog. And not a Chihuahua, either. More like a… well, like a Labrador. Some of my earth magic must have still been tangled in with my animal magic. He's sitting up on his hind legs, scratching his stomach and studying us.

"Shit," I whisper. Then I raise my voice. "Ratticus? You okay? You're not hurt, are you?"

Ratticus focuses on me, and his nose twitches. "You," he squeaks in a high, reedy voice.

"Did you hear that?" I mutter the question to Xander out of the corner of my mouth. "That wasn't a word, was it? Please tell me it was a perfectly normal rat noise."

Xander's mouth is hanging open. He closes it and swallows hard, his Adam's apple bobbing. "It sounded like a word." His shocked expression mirrors the way I feel.

I gulp down a rush of panic. "Ratticus, did you just speak?"

The rat blinks. "Speak." The word is high-pitched, but clear.

"Did he say *squeak*? He said *squeak*, right?" I don't know why I'm hoping Ratticus is just squeaking in English instead of rat language now. It's the thinnest of straws, but one I'm desperate to clutch.

Xander shakes his head. "You said talking rats were ridiculous. Remember? You said he'd need a bigger brain—"

"I remember." I don't want him to repeat our conversation in front of Ratticus, in case he now understands English. "I must have still had that in my mind when the animal magic was released, and it picked up on it." I give him a pointed look. "You said you'd seen stranger things than talking rats."

"I may have been mistaken." Xander scratches his chin. "So now you need to do another spell to turn him back to normal."

I press my lips together. Xander doesn't seem to understand how unlikely it is for any spell I do to go well. Watching me remove the chicken spell from Agnes has given him false expectations. I'd have thought watching me mess this spell up so badly might disillusion him, but apparently when it comes to my magic, his glasses have a stubbornly rose-colored hue.

"Hey," calls a voice from the top of the stairs. "Is everything okay? I was in the shower and heard some weird noises."

Jess. My roommate. Also, my best friend. Who doesn't know about witches or magic. Or giant talking rats.

After she's been out playing gigs with her band, she usually puts in ear plugs and sleeps late. If only she'd stayed in bed a little longer today.

I rush to the bottom of the stairs, flapping my hands at

Xander in the hopes he understands what I'm trying to communicate. Somehow, we have to keep Jess from seeing Ratticus.

"It was nothing." I force a smile that I hope looks casual. "No need to come down. We're fine."

Jess is dressed in her normal jeans and T-shirt, but has a towel wrapped around her wet hair. "Who's *we*?" she asks, starting down the stairs.

I look over to where Xander is herding Ratticus through the hall and into the laundry, and let out a sigh of relief. He must have understood my frantic hand gestures.

"Ah. Just me. And Xander. But there's no problem here. We're fine. No problem at all." I sound ridiculously guilty, like a cartoon villain, and I have an overpowering urge to smack myself on the forehead. But I'm too busy watching Xander push the giant rat into the laundry to be coherent.

He manages to get the door shut just as Jess reaches the bottom of the stairs. Then he leans against the door, his expression innocent.

Jess gives Xander a knowing look, as though his presence is the reason I'm acting so weird. "Hello, detective. You're visiting early. Or did you stay the night?" Before either of us can answer, she frowns, her gaze going from me to Xander and back again. "A bit early for Halloween, isn't it? What have you two been rolling around in?"

I exchange a glance with Xander. He's covered in dust. His clothes, his face, his hair, his eyebrows, and even his eyelashes are all light gray. He looks like a ghost.

I run my hand over my own hair and release a cloud of dust that makes me cough. Guess we're both ghosts.

"Xander was helping me decorate the courtyard," I say, making up a story off the top of my head. "I had an idea to give it a whole new look, but it turned out to be a dirty job."

"Oh-kay." She shakes her head, and I can tell she doesn't believe a word I just said. "Has all that hard work given you an appetite? I was thinking of making waffles."

I glance at Xander. "Thanks, Jess, but we already ate." Although, after all the meals we've missed over the last few days, I could do with some extra food. Spells are exhausting and I feel weak from the one I just did.

But we don't have time for more breakfast. Not with Ratticus in the laundry, and the council's deadline ticking quickly away.

Xander brushes at his filthy clothes and grimaces. "Mind if I wash up?"

As soon as he disappears up the stairs, Jess turns to me with wide, excited eyes, and makes a muffled screaming sound. "The hot detective stayed the night, didn't he? I want to know everything. Did he conduct a full and proper investigation of your body? Did you use handcuffs? How many times did he *take you down to the station?*" She uses her fingers to add quote marks to the last bit, as though I can't tell she's making up very lame euphemisms for sex.

I hold up both hands. "It wasn't like that. Nothing happened. We didn't even make it up to the bedroom."

"What? Why not?"

I shrug, wishing I could tell her the truth. "We were talking and fell asleep on the couch."

Her mouth drops open and she puts both hands on her hips. "You fell asleep on the couch?" she repeats in the same horrified tone she might use to describe a murder.

"We were tired." I'm trying not to sound defensive, but it's difficult when Jess is looking at me with such a shocked expression. "Anyway, what about you?" I ask. "Shouldn't something have happened between you and Mikey by now?"

Mikey's the bass player in The Flaming Buttholes. He and Jess have had crazy chemistry for years.

"Don't try to change the subject." She shakes her head sadly, as though I've let her down. "Seriously, it's about time you hooked up with someone nice, and it's obvious how much he likes you. He looks at you like he's a hungry lion and you're a fat goat with a broken leg."

I grimace at the graphic image. "Can we not talk about this anymore. Please?"

"Talk about what?"

I turn to see Xander coming back down the stairs, his face now clean, but his clothes still dusty.

I'm opening my mouth to say something that will distract him from his question when a tingling sensation ripples through my body. I taste something metallic and nasty in the back of my throat.

Before I have time to think about what I'm doing, I find myself striding toward the front door.

"Where are you going?" asks Xander.

I force my legs to stop and look back at him in confusion. "I'm not sure." The compulsion to keep walking to the door is getting stronger and stronger.

I'm not in control of my body any more. A putrid smell fills my nose, and I feel a slimy presence in the magic that's tingling against my skin.

A single red thread of magic extends from my chest to the door, and it's tugging at me, pulling me outside.

The Unseen.

He's cast a spell on me. He's forcing me to walk out of the house.

But how could he—?

Sudden realization squeezes my heart with fear. He

must be using the blood in my mother's ring to summon me. Why, oh why, did I ever let him take it?

I can't let him control me.

Clenching my fists, I grit my teeth and plant my feet on the ground, refusing to move although the compulsion is still pulling me.

Pain erupts in my chest. It's like a blunt axe is splitting my body in two.

I gasp, turning to Xander and Jess. I want to tell them what's happening and ask for help. But I can't. Jess has no idea about any of this, and if Xander finds out, he'll insist on coming with me. I can't let the Unseen find out the demon's moved in to Xander's body and is making itself at home. When the dark witch talked about Jeqabeel, there was a disturbing note of admiration in his voice. He'd find a way to take advantage of the demon being inside Xander, I'm sure of it.

No, I have to keep Xander away from him at all costs.

"Are you okay, Saff?" Xander takes the rest of the stairs two at a time.

"I'm fine." I manage to sound casual, though the compulsion to leave is too strong to control. "I just remembered that I need to head out for a little while. Sorry. I'll be back soon." As soon as I take a step toward the door, the pain in my chest eases a little.

"Now?" Jess's brow wrinkles with confusion. "You're going out all dirty?"

"Won't be long." Still walking, I shoot a reassuring smile over my shoulder, trying to pretend everything's normal. But my stomach is turning itself inside out and my mind is whirling.

I have less than forty-one hours to figure out how to save Xander. What if the Unseen kills me, or keeps me prisoner? What if I can't get away from him?

Should I really just walk out the door like nothing's wrong, when I might never see Jess or Xander again?

"Wait, Saffy." Xander follows me down the hallway to the door. "What's the matter? Tell me where you're going."

I bite the inside of my cheeks, forcing myself not to spill the beans. Last time we saw the Unseen, he called Xander a cockroach and asked if he could keep him. If I face the dark witch alone and find out what he wants, there's a chance I'll be able to get away quickly. But if Xander comes, I won't be able to protect him.

"I can't explain right now." I manage to get the words out almost normally. "But have waffles with Jess and I'll be back as soon as I can." I open the door, giving him another fake smile even as the pain in my chest increases again.

"I need to leave after breakfast," calls Jess. "I have band practice."

"If I'm not back by then, Xander will be okay here on his own. Right, Xander?" I shut the door without waiting for his answer and hurry to my pickup truck.

I can't fight the Unseen's spell, and I don't have time to waste. Not with the clock running down on Xander's life.

Chapter Three

Pulling up outside the Unseen's house, I vow to get my mother's ring back. It has to be the reason he can summon me like this. I should never have given it to him in the first place. Not that I had much of a choice.

The compulsion that pushes me out of my truck feels painful, like a million biting ants crawling over my body. I can still see the red strand of magic that's pulling me into the Unseen's house. It sucks that he can use my family's blood against me.

Stumbling toward his sweet-looking home—with its flowers, gnomes, and perfectly mowed lawn—makes bile rise in my throat. I keep trying to stop and turn back, but the closer I get to the Unseen, the stronger his summoning spell seems to get.

The defence wards the Unseen has around his house snag me briefly, sending the same unpleasant sensation over my skin as last time. But they release me quickly, and the front door creaks open before I can reach it.

He's expecting me, after all.

The hallway is empty, but I know the Unseen is in his basement because the thread of magic is leading me in that direction. My feet feel like they're operating without me, but I force them to stop at the top of the stairs that lead down to the basement. My heart pounds hard and my stomach contracts as I stare down into the black stairwell. The stench of his dark magic crawls up the stairs and infects my nostrils.

"Come, my dear. There's no point hesitating." The Unseen's grating voice floats up the stairs.

I take a deep breath, then another. I can do this. I'm strong.

Walking down the steps into inky blackness, I ignore the way my legs shake. The Unseen is standing beside his spell table at the back of the room, studying an open grimoire. He's bent and wizened, and his thin hair hangs dankly over his knobbly skull. The room is hot, and there are several bowls on his table filled with liquids. One is clearly full of blood, one smells like cat pee, and the other looks like it could be a bowl of porridge.

Behind the Unseen, an enormous stone statue looms. It's a horned creature with a hideously deformed head and a sinuous, eight-legged body. As ugly as it is, it's still better looking than the Unseen. His skin is even grayer than the last time I saw it and his face is covered with scabs, like he's been picking at his collection of sores. He's thin and bent over, with an old man's hunched posture.

I take a step forward, my hands clenched into fists. "What do you want?" I snarl.

The Unseen smiles, displaying his rotten teeth. The ones that aren't missing are sharpened to points. For a moment, I can't help staring; his mouth is a car wreck and I'm rubber necking. Then I wrinkle my nose with disgust and drag my gaze away.

"I want information." His voice is smug, and it's clear how much he's enjoying having me at his mercy.

"Information about what?"

"About Jeqabeel, of course."

"I don't know anything. And even if I did, I wouldn't tell you."

"Let me show you what I can do." He dips his index finger into his bowl of blood and draws a rune on the back of his hand. Quick and simple, the rune is a splash of brilliant red against the dull white of his skin. The magic glows red over his hand, and then more strands of magic curl toward me. I can't move back. The wisps of magic creep over me like fingers. Painful pins and needles erupt wherever they come in contact with my skin.

And just like that, my feet start moving again on their own, walking closer to him. Inside I'm yelling at them, ordering them to stop. But my body isn't my own.

A horrible compulsion to kiss the Unseen overcomes me. My lips purse, even as my stomach clenches in sick horror. I can't even make a noise, the scream I want to let out is trapped inside me. I'm really going to do it. I'm going to fasten my lips over his disgusting sewer of a mouth, and there's not a damn thing I can do to stop it.

But before I can reach him, the Unseen holds up the back of his hand with a gloating smirk, displaying the fact that half his pinky finger is missing. He wipes off the rune, smearing the blood with his fingers, and the compulsion to kiss him drops away.

I step back quickly, rubbing one shaking hand over my face. I feel like puking down the front of his stinking, old-man clothes. "If you ever do that again, I'll kill you."

His nasty smirk widens. "Then tell me what I want to know."

"Compulsion spells need strong animal magic. How

are you doing this?" He's an archivist, which means he can dabble with every type of magic, but only a witch with natural animal magic ability should be able to cast a spell that strong.

He tsks. "Your laws don't apply to me, Sapphira."

I flick a glance to the enormous bookshelves that cover the walls, with hundreds of books stacked inside them. The grimoires tremble with power, and he obviously studies their spells. I'm not entirely sure how dark magic works, but I know it gives him incredible power. He can probably do all kinds of things he shouldn't be able to.

One thing for sure, I'm not going tell him the demon's stuck inside Xander. Nor that the Blood Council made me drink their blood, joining me with them. Nor that my magic has been set free.

I press my lips into a tight line. It might not be easy to keep all that from him, but the less he knows, the better.

"I don't know anything about Jeqabeel," I say in a firm voice.

"There's also something else you can give me."

"The number of a good dentist?"

His face twists into a snarl. "I want the grimoire."

I look at him like I'm confused, but of course I know the one he means. The dark magic grimoire, written by the suicidal idiot who summoned Jeqabeel into our dimension in the first place. I wish I'd never shown the Unseen that damn book.

He narrows his eyes, hovering his fingers threateningly over his bowl of blood. "Don't play games with me. I can make you do things that will give you nightmares for the rest of your life."

I resist the urge to tell him his face has already done that. "Why do you want the grimoire?"

"It's becoming apparent that Jeqabeel has been

unleashed. There are now only two options open to us all. Either side with the demon, or die." To illustrate the two options, he waves his hand from one side to the other in front of him. As the collar of his shirt moves, I catch a glimpse of a faint red light glowing from underneath it.

With a shock I realize what it is. My mother's ring is on a chain around his neck. Her blood is encased in a crystal orb, and it's giving off a soft red glow.

"You want to help the demon?" My anger surges. Why the hell would anyone want to side with the thing that killed my parents and Sylvia? My magic rises as well, boiling hot and looking for release.

If the Unseen doesn't know the bonds restraining my magic have broken, maybe I could use it against him?

The only thing holding me back is the fear that my magic might make things worse. I don't exactly have a stellar track record. Ratticus's new vocal ability comes to mind.

"Jeqabeel can grant me anything I want," the Unseen snaps.

"Yeah?" I give him an exaggerated eye roll. "That would be so much cooler if Jeqabeel didn't have a weird demon fetish for destroying the world. In case you missed the memo, it gets off on killing people. Even if you help it, it'll destroy you too."

I'm itching to unleash my chaotic magic so I can try to slam it into his smug face. But I'm also scared that I might make him even more awful than he is now. How much more hideous would his face be if it were ten times bigger, like the dog I accidentally enlarged?

What if I accidentally made him even more powerful?

I can't take the risk. My magic is too out of control.

The Unseen shakes his head at me, his expression condescending. "The demon species is eminently rational, despite their desire for chaos. They can be bargained with, and their magic is intoxicating."

What the hell is it with crazy-ass witches wanting to be besties with terrifying demons out to destroy our world? The thought of Jeqabeel and the Unseen working together makes me shiver. It would be a match made in hell.

Now I know what the Unseen wants, it's even more important I find a way to get the demon out of Xander and either send it back where it came from, or lock it back up in an inanimate object. Having Uncle Ray acting as Jeqabeel's slave was bad enough. The Unseen's far more powerful, and if he's a card-carrying member of the jackal-demon appreciation club, he might succeed in feeding it the power it needs to murder a lot more people.

"Now that you've learned what I can do with your ring, I'm willing to offer you a trade," says the Unseen. "Bring me the grimoire and I'll give your ring back."

"Not going to happen." I give the ring around the Unseen's neck a glance that I hope seems casual. The fact that it's glowing proves that he's using it to control me. If I can yank it away from him, maybe I can escape with it and stop this madness.

Witches aren't usually physical. They're used to using magic, not their bodies. Whereas I've worked as a stone-mason for so many years, I can bench press my own body weight. Not to mention that I've survived enough Flaming Butthole concert mosh pits that I know how to take care of myself.

All I need to do is take him by surprise.

He shrugs. "You come from a long line of powerful witches, yet now I have you on a leash." He licks his tongue across the top of his revolting teeth and puts his fingers back over the bowl of blood. "Would you like another demonstration of my power? You're a very pretty girl,

Sapphira. I could make you do a lot more than just kiss me."

Rage floods over me. My magic, unable to release itself, boils through my veins. The stone magic feels heavy and powerful, while the animal magic is wild and violent. They clash against each other, both frantic to get free. With no blood to let them loose, they amplify my anger and push me into action.

Launching myself at the Unseen, I reach for the necklace that holds my mother's ring.

Chapter Four

The tips of my fingers brush against metal.

I have the necklace!

My heart soars as I fumble with it, trying to yank it from the Unseen's neck.

Snarling, the Unseen lifts one bloody hand. Red strands of magic snake toward me, and a heavy weight crushes me to the ground, flattening me against the stone floor with such force that I can't move.

"There's no way for you to get the better of me, Sapphira."

"Let me go." I try to claw my hand forward, but can barely lift my fingers.

With my face pressed hard against the stone floor of the basement, I can't see the Unseen. But I feel his magic build again, its terrible power prickling my skin. My body lifts off the floor, then I fly across the room. I slam hard into a bookcase and drop to the floor. Grimoires fall around me. I want to groan with pain, but first I have to fight to recover the breath that's been knocked out of me.

One of the grimoires is open on the floor, its pages showing a drawing of a snake. A spell is scrawled underneath the drawing, written in a language I can't decipher. Its words pulse and writhe on the page.

The Unseen cackles. "My dear, compared to me, you're as weak as a newborn. You'll bring me the grimoire, or you'll die. It's that simple."

Grimly, I push myself back to my feet. My back aches where I slammed into his bookcase. "I don't have the dark magic grimoire. I lost it." I motion to the books that have fallen around me. "If you have a Veritas truth spell in there somewhere, use it to prove I'm not lying."

His face twists into an ugly snarl. "Then you'll find the grimoire," he snaps. "And until you bring it to me, you'll be my spy. Jeqabeel is gathering strength in this dimension, preparing to take on his own physical form. I want to know what the Blood Council's doing to stop him."

I drop my gaze to the floor at the mention of the council. He can't know I've been forced to join their ranks, and I don't want anything to show on my face.

"I've been hidden in plain sight, right under the council's nose for years." He smirks. "I'm not about to attract its attention now. You will be my eyes and ears. When you come back with the grimoire, you'll tell me their plans."

"I'm an outsider too. Most other witches hate me. I won't be able to find out anything useful." I can't stop the bitter edge to my words.

"Your Uncle Ray is a council member. You'll learn everything he knows."

His mention of Uncle Ray makes me falter for a second. "And if I don't?" I ask. After all, it's not like I can actually spy on my uncle any more.

The Unseen dips one finger into his bowl of blood and

draws a rune on his other palm. Dark magic swells out from the rune and covers me in its greasy strands. My mother's ring glows even brighter.

This time I'm locked in place. I can't move at all. My arms are fixed at my sides and I can't even blink. I growl deep in my throat, but it doesn't help.

Smirking, the Unseen steps closer to me. "I wasn't sure how much power over you the ring would give me, but I'm rather pleased." He moves around to my side where I can't see him, and whispers in my ear. "You have no choice but to obey me."

His warm breath on my lobe makes me shudder in revulsion. At least, I wish I could shudder. My body won't even obey me that much.

"You'll go to your uncle and find out what the council knows about Jeqabeel's return, or I'll make your life very unpleasant." He licks my neck below my ear, and one of his calloused fingers runs down the bare skin of my arm.

I scream with fury, pounding my fist repeatedly into his face. Unfortunately, no noise actually emerges from my mouth, and my arm refuses to so much as twitch.

"If you disobey me, I'll destroy everything you hold dear. And I'll enjoy it."

He walks back in front of me, palm held up to show me the rune. Then he closes his fingers over the top part of it. The spell releases from my head so I can move it, though the rest of my body is still frozen.

"Now, I expect an answer. Will you obey?"

I suck in a breath, not sure how to answer. The only thing I can say is the truth. Part of it, anyway.

"I can't ask Uncle Ray anything," I blurt. "He's dead."

"What? How?"

"The council killed him," I lie outright. I don't need

him knowing what really happened. "And they banished the demon back into its bone, so you can forget about being Jeqabeel's boy toy."

"You're lying." He picks up a knife from his spell table and turns it left and right. It gleams in the dim light. "But I can teach you to tell the truth."

He walks back over to me, and though I strain with all my strength, I can't move away. All I can do is jerk my head back as he presses the knife against my cheek. "You're my slave. I can do whatever I like to you."

I grind my teeth, too furious to answer.

Then the Unseen grasps my hand in his. "This will make our connection even stronger," he whispers. I feel a moment of relief as he pulls the knife away from my face. Then he cuts into my palm. I cry out and my magic surges.

For a brief moment, I'm exultant. He's unknowingly set my magic free. I can slam it into him. Maybe if I think about slugs, I can turn him into one.

Only… my magic isn't blasting out of me like runaway rockets on the Fourth of July. The spell he's using to control me is holding my magic in too. It's seething and battering against his restraints, but it can't get free.

I take a shaky breath as the Unseen holds up his knife, my blood dripping down the edge of the blade. What's he going to do with my blood? He's already got me completely locked in place. What more is he planning?

The Unseen slides his tongue along the knife's blade and licks my blood. All at once, I feel the connection between us deepen. Now it's like a heavy, suffocating blanket clinging to me, sucking on my energy. Its cloying feel is so disgusting it makes my stomach churn.

The Unseen's eyes widen. "I can taste... You've joined the Blood Council. I feel their connection in your blood."

He smiles, showing me his mouth full of sharpened teeth, and his eyes glitter. "This is a valuable gift. Through you, I'll be able to draw on the council's power."

He steps away, licking the other side of the knife, as though my blood is so delicious, he wants to lap up every drop.

Bile claws its way up my throat, and I gag.

I try to clench my fists, and I'm surprised when I manage it. The spell he cast is weakening. And my blood is still dripping from the cut in my palm. Any minute the Unseen will figure out that the bindings around my own magic are gone. I have to act fast, but that horrible blanket of control is still clinging to me.

I concentrate on the wound, on forcing my magic to seep out with my blood. It oozes from my veins, sneaking through the dampening effect of the Unseen's control. As violently as it wants to get out, it's like viscous fluid being forced through tiny holes, leaching quietly through the barrier.

Hope flares inside me.

His magic isn't as all-consuming as he thinks. My stone magic is seeping into the cobbles at our feet, and it's stronger now that it's found purchase inside its natural element. I have to act fast, before he realises my magic is free.

I push my earth magic into the cobbles with everything I've got.

A rumbling noise growls through the basement, and the stones beneath our feet move and shift. The creepy stone statue in the corner of the room rocks slowly back and forth as the stones undulate beneath it.

"What are you doing?" The Unseen staggers backward, his knife clattering to the ground.

The cobblestone under his feet bucks violently,

throwing him sideways onto his table. His bowl of blood goes flying, splattering red all over the Unseen, as well as the floor and table. All at once, his hold over me snaps and I'm free from his spell.

My animal magic explodes out of me like water from a burst hydrant. It pours itself gleefully into the open grimoire on the ground by the bookcase. An animal magic grimoire, I realize.

The snake drawn on the open page starts moving, slithering out from the paper, becoming a real snake in full three-dimensional colour. As it emerges from the grimoire, it somehow starts to swell, expanding in size from the tiny drawing into an enormous serpent, its body thicker than my waist.

But it doesn't stop there; the snake keeps growing, doubling and then tripling in size. It already seems impossibly long, and more and more of the snake's body is emerging from the grimoire. It lifts its head to the ceiling, its long tongue flickering as it tastes the air. Its body is growing so fast, it bumps against me, pushing me back against the wall.

Its massive blue-green coils are filling the basement, crashing into the shelves, knocking over bottles and crushing vials. Its head is now the size of a single bed and if I stick around, its huge body will crush me.

The Unseen screeches, but I can't see him anymore. The room is too full of snake, and still more keeps pouring out of the book.

Scrambling awkwardly over giant snake coils, I manage to make it to the bottom of the stairs. I glance back, wondering how the Unseen will deal with the snake. Then I shrug to myself, and run up the stairs and out the front door.

It's not until I'm in my truck and halfway home that my

thumping heart slows down, and I realise my mother's ring is still around the Unseen's neck.

Chapter Five

When I stop my pickup truck outside my house, my hands are still shaking. It's almost one o'clock, so I've been gone a couple of hours. Two hours wasted, and Xander doesn't have enough time left that I can afford to let a single minute slip by.

There's blood on the steering wheel from the cut on my palm, and it feels sticky. I switch the engine off and drag in a breath. Not long ago, my house was warded, which meant it was safe from any magic users that meant to cause me harm. Now, thanks to the dogs my uncle sent to attack me, the wards are gone.

With no wards, the Unseen can control me again any time he likes.

I hurry through the gate to my front door. When I get inside, I smell coffee and waffles, and the tension in my chest eases a little. In spite of the house being unwarded, I still feel safer here. My home has always been my refuge, and I refuse to let the Unseen take that away from me. As much as I hate having anything to do with them, I'll have to ask the council to help me set up new protection wards to keep him and his slimy spells out.

I follow my nose into the kitchen, where Xander is drinking coffee at the kitchen table, an empty plate in front of him. I'm so glad to see him, it takes a Herculean effort not to rush over and throw my arms around him in spite of the demon.

He looks up, his eyebrows raised. "You were gone longer than I thought. And you took your truck." His eyes are asking the question that he's not asking in words.

I let out a long breath. "Jess has gone to band practise?"

He nods.

"Where's Ratticus?" I ask. "Still in the laundry?"

"Um." Xander stands up. "About that. Slight problem."

I follow him to the hallway. He opens the laundry door and I look inside. The room is empty, and the window over the washing tub is broken. Out in the courtyard, the enormous dog statue is every bit as ugly as I remember. It looms over the destroyed paving stones, taking up most of the small space.

Agnes the chicken was trapped in the courtyard for several days, unable to get free. Ratticus clearly didn't have that problem. There's a Labrador-sized hole in the fence.

I stare at Xander in horror. "He escaped?"

Xander nods. "We were eating when we heard a crash. Jess came rushing out, and I tried to stop her from looking in the laundry, but she dodged past me and threw open the door. We found it like this. Empty."

"Perfect." I rub my uninjured hand over my face, wishing I could curl up in a corner of my bedroom and never come out. "Did Jess say anything about the statue?"

"Only four-letter words."

"What did you tell her about it?"

"Nothing. When she asked how it got there, I played dumb. It wasn't hard."

"Okay. Good." I'm determined to stay calm even though I'm drowning in problems. "When Jess gets back, I'll make up a story to explain the statue. Did you go out and look for Ratticus yet?"

He nods. "As soon as Jess left, I searched up and down the street. There's no sign of him."

"Shit," I breathe softly.

He nods again. "Anyone who sees him is going to get a hell of a surprise."

"No kidding. As soon as I leave, he manages to escape. Damn rat."

"Where did you go, anyway?" Xander's sharp eyes are on me.

I shake my head, not wanting to share yet another problem. He's already under so much pressure, and I need him to stay positive. Besides, I'm not sure I can tell him about the Unseen without breaking down.

"You look pale." He puts his hand out to touch my arm, seems to remember at the last minute that he can't touch me, and shoves his hands in his pocket. "Want a waffle?" he asks.

I nod wordlessly. He leads me back to the kitchen, where he pulls out a chair for me at the kitchen table. "I can tell something bad happened while you were out. You need to tell me about it. We can't afford to have any more secrets."

I move to the table, but I'm feeling too jumpy to sit down. He's right, as much as I want to protect him, there's no point in keeping him in the dark. Not when the Unseen could pull me away again at any moment.

"Remember how the Unseen took my mother's ring

instead of the grimoire? It's given him power over me. He compelled me to go to him and I couldn't stop myself from doing it." I say the words in a rush, as if getting them out fast will make them less… terrible.

"He can do that?" Xander pulls a face. "Obviously he can."

"He can, and he did." I clench my fists in an effort to stop my hands trembling.

"Are you okay?"

"I'm fine," I say, even though I'm really not.

"What did he want?"

"He wanted to know about Jeqabeel, and he wanted me to give him the dark magic grimoire. He wasn't happy when I told him I didn't have it anymore."

"You should have told me where you were going. I would have come with you. I could have helped."

My sigh is small. "And have the Unseen, a powerful dark witch, discover he can access Jeqabeel through you?"

"I wouldn't have let him find out." He pulls the foil off a plate of waffles, then puts it on the kitchen table. He and Jess saved me some. Shame my stomach is scrunched into a tight ball.

"The Unseen now knows that I'm on the Blood Council and that Uncle Ray's dead," I slide into the seat in front of the plate of waffles. "He wants to help the demon get its own form. That's a very good reason not to let you near him."

"You shouldn't have gone there alone." His eyebrows draw together.

Something inside me snaps. "I didn't have a choice," I say too loudly. "He forced me there. He can make me do things I don't want to do." Swallowing, I push the plate of waffles away.

"I'm sorry." Xander takes a step toward me, then folds

his arms as though he needs to make a conscious effort to stop himself from touching me. "Are you really okay?"

"I'm fine. I escaped." I watch the muscles move over Xander's crossed forearms, and desperately wish he could hug me right now.

"He didn't hurt you, did he?"

I sniff the air. "Is something burning?"

"Dammit!" Xander jerks the oven open and pulls out black strips of something that might once have been bacon. "I was keeping it warm." He glowers at the blackened mess.

"It doesn't matter. The waffles will be nice with syrup." I pull the plate of waffles back toward me and pour some syrup on top of the stack. Ignoring the unpleasant way my stomach's churning, I take a bite. If my mouth's full, he can't expect me to answer questions.

Xander runs his hand through his hair like he does whenever he's frustrated. "I understand why you didn't want to tell me he could to compel you to go to him, but I hate the thought of you having to go back to his house alone. Even knowing it would have been risky, I wish I'd been there with you."

"It's nice to know you have my back." Surprisingly, the waffle is sliding down okay. I take another bite.

"You said you escaped. How'd you get away?"

"Giant snake."

"Really?" He sounds impressed.

"Long story, but I conjured it out of a drawing."

"That sounds cool."

"Totally bad-ass," I agree. Even if I did it by accident.

"You think if I sketch a picture of Jeqabeel locked up in another piece of bone, you could magically make it happen?"

"If only."

He lets out a sigh. "Well, it was worth asking. Art's not really my thing, but I bet I could have come up with a really creative drawing. My version of his bone prison would have sharp nails. Maybe barbed wire. And that God-awful music you like, playing on continuous repeat for the next thousand years."

Amazingly enough, I manage an almost-smile. Being with Xander, talking things through with him, makes me feel a lot better.

"Just tell me one thing. Did the snake eat the Unseen?" The relish in Xander's voice makes my smile a little more genuine.

"I ran out of there, so I don't know what happened. But his magic is pretty powerful. He probably made the snake go boom." I cut another, larger piece of waffle. "I just hope he ends up with so much snake goo splattered over his basement, it takes him forever to clean up."

"If only he'd drown in it," mutters Xander.

I nod with my mouth full. My appetite is coming back and the waffles are starting to taste pretty damn good.

"You want more coffee to wash that down?" Xander gets up. "Or some juice?"

"Juice, please." Now my shakes are disappearing, my mind is starting to work again. We have less than thirty-eight hours before the council summons Xander back. As abhorrent as the Unseen is, that makes him second on my list of priorities.

As Xander puts a glass of juice in front of me, I say, "I think you're right. We should get the dark magic grimoire back. It might have some answers."

"Your uncle used the grimoire when he killed Sylvia, didn't he?" Xander sounds thoughtful.

I nod. "He used it to pull out her magic."

"Perhaps we can use it to weaken the demon. Extract that magic back out of Jeqabeel."

"Maybe it'll tell us how to send the demon back where it came from." I put down my knife and fork, liking this plan more and more. "Besides, the Unseen really wanted to get his hands on the grimoire. If nothing else, we can lock it back in Sylvia's athenaeum to keep it safe from him."

"You think—?"

A high-pitched ring goes off, and I jump. It's the phone in the living room. No one ever rings it. I'm not even sure why we keep it connected.

I run to answer it, then hesitate with my hand over the cradle. Who could it be? Uncle Ray used to ring me on this line occasionally, but that's about it. Now that he's dead, it should be a ghost line. I don't have a whole heap of admirers itching to chat.

There's only one way to find out.

"Hello?"

"Oh, thank God," says Jess, her voice tinny and distant. "Saffy, you have to come and get me. I don't know what happened. I'm cold. I didn't know I could be this cold. Please, Saffy, I need you to come right now." Jess is sobbing into the phone, making her words difficult to understand. But one thing comes across loud and clear—she's terrified.

My stomach turns over. Could the Unseen have done something to her? Or the Blood Council? "Jess, what's happened? Where are you?" I glance at Xander who's followed and is hovering over me, his expression worried.

"Just come quickly." Her voice wobbles, and even over the phone line, I can tell she's close to the edge.

"Tell me where you are." Blood is pumping through my veins, fear making my heart work overtime. I've never heard Jess sound afraid before. She's hard core, always leaping into fights without a care for her own safety. She's been arrested a few times, and has even been to jail.

"I'm on the corner of Jones and Memorial." The line goes dead.

I hang up and turn to Xander. "We have to get Jess."

"What did she say?"

"She's in trouble." I stride to the door. "Come on."

Chapter Six

I glance at my watch. It's taken almost forty-five minutes to get to the corner of Jones and Memorial. Time we don't have to waste with the council's spell ticking down.

But this is Jess. I can't leave her hanging.

She's standing back from the corner, half hidden in the shadows. Xander pulls over, and I leap out and run to her. She's weeping, the tears creating tracks down her dirty face. Her shirt's been ripped, and her jeans have a jagged tear just below the knee. She must have fallen over, because she's skinned her knee and there's dried blood on her jeans.

"Jesus, Jess! What the hell happened? Who did this to you?" I gather her into my arms, trying to comfort her. "Where are the rest of the Buttholes?"

She just shakes her head and collapses against me, her whole body shaking with sobs. For the first time since I've known her, she feels small and frail.

My arms tighten around her and I move her toward the car. Between us, Xander and I manage to get her into the back seat and belted up. I slip in next to her. Jess is still shaking against me.

I'm going to kill whoever hurt her.

"Let's get out of here," I say to Xander who's already turning the key in the ignition.

"What happened?" He meets my gaze in the rear vision mirror as he pulls away.

Jess is too busy crying to talk, and doesn't seem to hear the question. I shake my head.

Who could possibly want to hurt her? Everyone loves her. And her band mates in the Flaming Buttholes would never let anything bad happen to her. Wracking my brain, the only thing I can think of is that she occasionally works with some dodgy people, stripping stolen cars for parts. Could she have rubbed one of them the wrong way? Maybe seen something she shouldn't?

The other possibility is a lot worse. What if someone hurt Jess to get at me? Is this something the Unseen might have done, as revenge for the snake? If he's responsible, I won't rest until he's stopped.

For the entire return journey, I keep my arms around Jess, trying to comfort her. I force myself not to look at my watch again, but the feeling of time slipping through our fingers is hard to ignore. Everything seems to be going against us.

In the front seat, Xander looks calm, but his hands are clenched tight on the steering wheel, and his jawline looks razor-sharp. He's just as worried as I am.

Jess is clearly distraught. The only wound I can find is her skinned knee, and at least it's stopped bleeding. I manage to wipe some of the dirt out of the cut flesh with a corner of my T-shirt, though she whimpers as I'm doing it. I can't get her to say anything.

Xander parks the car, and between us we get Jess into

the house and up the stairs to her room. She sits down on the bed, her face dirty and pale, her body hunched over.

"Will you make her a hot milk?" I ask Xander as I pull Jess's shoes off. Maybe she'll talk to me if he's not in the room.

He gives me a sharp look, then nods and goes out.

Jess still has a leaf in her hair, and I pull it out and frown at it, wishing it could talk so it could tell me what the hell happened to her. Stroking my hand over her head, I check for any other foreign objects. "What happened, Jess?" I gently lift her face, trying to get her to look me in the eyes, but she's only half awake, unable to even talk. Whatever it was, it's left her bone-tired.

"Come on," I say with a sigh. "We have to get you cleaned up. I can't put you to bed like this."

She groans, but lets me pull her up and drag her to the bathroom. I get her under the shower and wash the worst of the dirt off her, before helping her into her warmest PJs.

Then I roll up one leg and pull out the first aid kit out so I can clean and bandage the wound on her knee. I wish my magic wasn't so messed up, so I could heal it for her and relieve the pain. Instead I dab on some antiseptic, just like an ordinary mundane.

Finally, I let Jess crawl into bed. Xander has left a mug of hot milk on her bedside table, but I doubt Jess will drink it.

When I pull the covers up to her chin, she sighs, snuggling down further into bed.

"Are you ready to talk about it?" I sit on the bed beside her. I need to know how she managed to get to a place so far from where her band was practicing, and where her car is. None of it makes sense.

"I don't know what happened, Saff. I was at practice and then I wasn't." She rolls onto her side, bringing her knees up under the covers. Her eyes are doing slow blinks, like they really want to stay closed.

I frown. "You were playing drums? Then what did you do?"

"We were on a break, and I went outside for some fresh air." On the next blink, her eyes don't open.

"What happened then?"

"That's the part I don't know," she mumbles.

"Do you remember anyone approaching you? Were you knocked out? Did you fall?"

"I think I fell. Tripped over." She lets out a long breath, her voice fading fast. "I'm exhausted, Saff. Can we talk about it later?"

"Okay." I squeeze her shoulder before standing up. "Jess, I'm really sorry but I need to go out again. I'm going to call Mikey to come and stay with you, okay?"

She gives a sleepy nod, and I can only hope she's taking in what I'm saying. I wish I had time to sit here with her, to watch over her while she sleeps and make sure she's safe. But I'm too conscious of how few hours Xander has left.

I find her cellphone in her jeans pocket. She has three missed calls, all from Mikey, and I hover over her, listening to her soft breathing, while I use her phone to call him back.

"Jess," he says when he answers. He sounds relieved, and the loud music playing in the background abruptly cuts off. "Where'd you go? We've all been worried."

"It's Saffy," I speak quietly because Jess already looks like she's asleep. "Would you come over to our place? Jess isn't well and I don't want her to be alone."

"What the hell's going on?" His tone is sharp. "We thought she was going outside for a five minute break. Why'd she take off?"

"I don't know what happened. She's in bed, and I have to go out for an hour or two."

"In bed? Is she okay?"

"She's sleeping. I tried to get her to talk, but she was too upset, and she seems a little confused. It'd be great if you could stay with her."

"I'm on my way. Be there in ten." Mikey sounds a little breathless, like he's already rushing to his car. The worry in his voice makes me feel a little better about having to leave. Mikey's been in love with Jess for years, and I know she'll be in good hands until I get back.

"Jess, are you still awake?" I whisper when I hang up. "Mikey's coming to look after you."

She grunts softly, but I'm not sure how much she's taking in. I program Xander's number into her cellphone and leave it on her nightstand. "Call Xander's number if you need anything. I'll be back as soon as I can." She doesn't reply, and I let myself out of her room, shutting the door softly behind me.

Xander is waiting in the hallway. "Is she asleep?"

I nod. "She was out like a light." When we go downstairs, I wince at the grandfather clock in the hallway. Time seems like it's rushing past faster and faster, and I've done nothing to help Xander. "The lead singer of her band will be here in a few minutes. As soon as he gets here, we can go and look for the grimoire."

"I'll make coffee while we wait."

I follow him into the kitchen, but I'm too wired to sit down. Instead I pace back and forth, watching him use the coffee maker to froth milk.

"Tell me about Jess," he says over the noise of the machine. "Has anything like this ever happened to her before?"

"Not that I know of. Maybe she hit her head."

"Is she a witch?"

"No. She's as mundane as you are."

"How long have you known her?"

I shrug. "Depends how you define it. I saw her playing with the Flaming Buttholes a few times. She's a great drummer. But I didn't actually get to know her until she moved in with me, and pretty much saved my life."

He looks over his shoulder at me and raises his eyebrows. "Saved your life?"

"You should have seen my house. It was half destroyed after the explosion. Entire walls were missing, and my parents had both died inside. I still can't believe she agreed to move in."

"It's strange that she did," he agrees. His eyes are sharp, and I can practically hear his detective brain ticking. Even when there's no mystery, he's determined to figure everything out.

"If it weren't for her, I wouldn't have been able to pay any of my bills," I tell him. "I might have lost the house and had to live on the street. She's a life saver. I'm not exaggerating."

"And you're good friends now?" He slides a mug of coffee across the counter toward me.

"The best." I shake my head. "You drink the coffee. I can't stomach anything right now."

He picks up the mug. "So she'd tell you if she'd experienced something like this before? What happened today, I mean."

"Of course she would."

He lifts the mug to his lips, but hesitates without taking a sip. I have the feeling his detective brain has come up with a possible solution. Typical Xander. His own life is in danger, yet he's trying to figure out the answer to somebody else's problem.

"Did you solve the crime, Sherlock?" I ask.

"I was just wondering if the Unseen could be responsible for whatever happened to her today."

My stomach drops. "You think he would go after Jess?" He's saying my worst fear out loud, and it's scary to know his thoughts have been going in the same direction as mine.

"Probably. He has it in for you."

A loud rapping comes from the front door, and I jump, my heart skipping. But it's not like the Unseen would knock. It's got to be Mikey.

Sure enough, when I open the door, Mikey's outside, looking as worried as he sounded on the phone. His band T-shirt is faded to gray, and a colorful snake tattoo curls down one of his arms, reminding me of the snake I pulled out of the Unseen's grimoire.

"Thanks for coming," I say. "Jess is upstairs, in bed."

"She tell you what happened?" As Mikey comes in, he notices Xander behind me and frowns, his gaze suspicious. "Hey. Who are you?"

"Xander." Shifting his mug of coffee to his left hand, the detective sticks out his right hand, offering to shake. "I'm a friend of Saffy's."

"Oh." His brow smooths, the hint of jealousy fading from his expression as soon as he learns Xander is my friend rather than Jess's. "I'm Mike."

But just as Mikey steps forward to take Xander's hand, the detective whips his hand away. He's obviously just remembered he shouldn't touch anyone.

Mikey's frown comes back and his gaze goes to me. "What exactly—?"

"Sorry, we can't talk now." I step past him, heading out the door. "Come on, Xander. We need to leave."

"But did Jess say why she left band practise?"

"We have no answers." Xander follows me outside, still holding his coffee. "Hopefully she'll tell us more when she wakes up. In the meantime, don't let anyone in the house. Not for any reason. And if you need to call us, my number is in Jess's cellphone." He's using his detective voice, making it sound like an order, and Mikey bristles.

"Why would I call you and not Saffy?" he demands.

"I broke my phone." I give him a wave as I climb into Xander's car. "Take good care of Jess, okay?"

I'm still upset by the thought the Unseen might have hurt my best friend, so when Xander plays Frank Sinatra on the car stereo the whole way to the library, I don't even object.

Xander pulls into a parking place near the library, and switches the engine off. "The library's closed," he says, peering at the building. "And there's a security guard posted on the door. "How do you plan to get past him?"

"We'll ask him to let us in."

He stares at me, eyebrows raised. "That's your brilliant plan? We're going to ask a security guard not to do the job he's being paid for?"

"Haven't you ever blagged your way through security using your badge? You're the great detective Xander Trent, aren't you? He might be so in awe of you that he can't wait to let you in."

"Uh, there might be a tiny flaw in that plan." He holds his finger and thumb close together to illustrate how small it is. "They took my badge away. We're fugitives, and there's probably a warrant out for our arrest." He gets out of the car and slams the door a little too hard.

I jump out too, frowning at his expression. "We're innocent. I can ask the council to take care of it once the demon is sorted. They can probably get your badge back." I make my tone confident and reassuring, though I'm anything but. The thought of asking the Blood Council for help gives me a bad taste in my mouth. But Xander's lost so much because of me.

He shakes his head. "It's just that a week ago, I was a detective, and I worked damn hard to get there. Now I'm a criminal with a demon inside me that could wipe out the entire city."

I wince. If he'd never met me, he'd still be a detective. "Sorry."

His mouth twists. "Not your fault. But the worst part of all of this is that I can't touch you." He drags his hand through his hair. "And I'm getting really sick of listening to the demon whispering in my head."

I want to ask what the demon's saying, but I'm pretty sure I already know. Instead, I follow him to the library's entrance.

The security guard watches us silently. He was leaning against the side of the building next to the door, but he pushes off from it and stands straighter when we get close.

"Morning," Xander sounds brisk. "I'm Detective Trent, and this is Ms. Black. She's an antiquities expert. We're here to inspect the artefacts that were damaged in the… incident."

Dammit, I should have thought to change into something more professional looking than jeans and a black Death Metal T-shirt. At least I managed to get most of the paving stone dust out of my hair.

I nod, my expression serious, and try to look intelligent while the guard examines me doubtfully.

"You know the building's unstable?" he says. "I've been instructed to keep everyone at a safe distance, in case it collapses."

I blink, trying to hide my shock. How badly did my

magic damage the building? I've always loved the George Peabody Library. If it falls down, I'll never forgive myself.

"So I was told," says Xander. "But there are priceless items in there, and Ms. Black is the only one who can safely catalog them. I'm sure they let you know to expect us?"

The guard shakes his head. "First I've heard of it."

"I know you're just doing your job, but we've been fully briefed on the risks, and we've already signed the release forms. If I need to get further authorisation, that'll waste everyone's time."

I let out a quiet sigh. This isn't going to work. Maybe I could try doing a spell to make the guard think we're—

"Okay," says the guard with a shrug. He steps aside, waving us to the door. "Just don't take too long. And if you bring anything out with you, I'll need to call it in."

Xander and I exchange a quick glance, then hustle our butts through the door before he changes his mind.

We cross the lobby, hurry through the exhibition galley, and go into the main part of the library. It's a spectacular room with a tall central atrium encircled by five floors of books. It's one of the most beautiful libraries in the world, a book-lover's cathedral.

Now I can only wince at the devastation.

Sunlight shines through the skylight high above us, picking out the mess in bright golden detail. One entire section of the library has been completely destroyed, all five floors collapsed to the ground. Thousands of books litter the floor of the central foyer, along with the remains of the bookcases, wrought-iron balustrades, and ornate marble columns. Large cracks run up the library's walls, and rubble is everywhere.

The library used to be my favorite place to visit, and it hurts my heart to see it ruined. But I don't have time to mourn for it. The knee-deep ocean of books will make it much harder to find the one that'll get us into the magical part of the library.

With difficulty, I wade through the devastation until I reach the far corner of the lower floor. Thankfully, this isn't the section of the library that collapsed, so it's not buried in rubble. But all the stacks have toppled, making it a challenge to find the right one. When I get close to where I think the portal is, I take a deep breath and close my eyes, searching for the tingle of magic.

There.

I plough forward, tripping over debris, hunting through the piles of fallen books. The one I'm looking for has a powerful protection ward, and I make my fingers push through its resistance until I find the source of the power.

"Got it," I exclaim, holding up the book. "Harry Potter and the Chamber of Secrets."

When I flip open the book, the portal appears. Usually it looks like a hole opening up in the bookcase, but with the bookcase on the floor, the portal hovers in mid-air. It's even more mind-bending than usual.

"I'll never get used to that," mutters Xander. Still, he follows me through the black hole, and we walk down the spiral staircase that leads into the Witch Library.

As we head into the bowels of the building, we hear creaking, like the library is moving on its foundations. "It doesn't seem very stable." I whisper the words because it feels like speaking too loudly might shake the building enough to make it collapse on us.

"Let's move faster," he agrees.

I speed up the pace, going down two steps at a time. The stone gargoyle that gave us so much trouble last time is waiting at the bottom of the stairs.

"Who seeks entry?" it asks.

"Sapphira Black and Xander Trent."

I brace myself to have another argument with it. But maybe it remembers us from last time we were here. Or perhaps it senses the demon that's hiding in Xander, and Jeqabeel's presence creeps out the gargoyle as much as it does me. Either way, the wall behind it shimmers and dissolves.

The Witch Library is dark and silent. I can feel the power of the books but I can't see far into the room. The only light comes from the stairwell behind us, and beyond it is pitch black.

"Can you use your magic to create some light?" whispers Xander.

"Unfortunately, I'd need fire magic to do that. But if you need any more talking rats, I'm your girl." Stepping forward, I peer into the darkness. "Where do you suppose the light switch is?" As my eyes start to adjust, I can see some of the shelves we knocked over are still on the floor, and the books are scattered. I guess the building's too unstable for anyone to have bothered straightening up.

The dark magic grimoire will probably be among those books. I'm pretty sure I lost it when the demon threw me onto the stacks.

I start forward. Then I catch a flash of light from the other side of the room. "Did you see that?" I whisper, stopping dead.

"Someone else is here." Xander's voice is a low murmur, aimed near my ear. His breath tickles the sensitive skin on my neck.

I blink, trying to concentrate. "It seems weird they'd be using a flashlight instead of turning on the main lights." With Xander right next to me, I can pick up the faintly woody scent of his skin. Even after all we've been through, and with a demon inside him, he still smells good. He's so close, it feels impossibly cruel that we can't actually touch.

"Maybe the power's out, and they needed an important book," he whispers.

"A book emergency?" I shake my head. "Something feels off."

"Let's go over there."

We feel our way through the shelves, creeping quietly toward the light. By mutual unspoken agreement, we avoid the area where we found the dead librarian. The light's coming from the restricted area, where the more potent grimoires are kept. Not a good sign.

Together we peer around the edges of the stacks.

A man is sitting at one of the long tables, using his flashlight to read. The book he has is an ancient-looking grimoire, and I bet it's one of the dangerous ones that are usually kept locked up. The power it gives off makes all the hairs on my arms stand on end.

The man turns the page, and the light reflects up to his face. I gasp. "It's Dallas."

Chapter Seven

"What's Dallas doing here?" whispers Xander.

"Looking up dangerous spells, apparently." I murmur back.

Dallas's head snaps up and he shines the flashlight in our direction. We both shrink back into the shadows, but I knock my hip into the side of the stack, and the muffled thump seems loud in the silence.

"Who's there?" Dallas stands up, sweeping the room with his flashlight.

"It's just me." I motion for Xander to stay hidden. Dallas hates me, but Xander's the one he's more likely to want to hurt. He argued pretty hard to have Xander killed and was furious when Magnus decided to give us forty-eight hours to get the demon out of him.

I step toward Dallas, squinting at the blinding light he shines into my eyes, and holding my hands out like I'm a hostage negotiator. "I didn't think anyone else would be here. I just wanted to do some research on the demon."

"Don't bother," he snarls. "The only way to trap it is to

turn your boyfriend into stone before the demon has time to consume him from the inside."

I shake my head. "I won't let the council do that."

Dallas makes a growling sound in the back of his throat. "You shouldn't get a say in it. You're not even a proper witch."

He lowers the flashlight from my face so I can see him. In the weird light, his face is made up of dramatic horror-movie dark and light patches. His mouth is contorted, and he looks more than a little crazy.

"I'm sorry, Dallas." I try to make my voice soothing. "I understand you're upset. I've lost people too. But killing Xander won't bring Mireya back. What happened to her was—"

Dallas drops the flashlight and throws both arms in the air like a gymnast after a somersault. Strands of his magic fill the air, and wind suddenly builds, swirling around me and whipping my hair into my face. Some of the books fall from the shelves, their pages flapping.

I take a step backward. "Dallas, what are you doing?"

"How dare you say her name? Mireya was worth ten— no, one hundred—of you. You should have died, not her." He flings both hands toward me and a blast of wind hits me, so strong it almost feels solid. I fly backward, my arms spread out. My back slams into the end of a library stack, and the breath whooshes out of my lungs. My legs collapse and I slump to the floor.

In the light from the fallen flashlight, I catch a shadow rushing from behind the stacks. It's Xander. He runs at Dallas and shoves him backward.

Like most witches who rely heavily on magic, Dallas isn't very strong. He staggers back, stumbles, and hits the floor. Then he scrambles back up to his feet.

"When you touched me with your filthy demon hands,

it tried to *possess* me," Dallas spits, outrage making his voice shrill. "You shouldn't be allowed to walk around."

Xander takes a step toward him, then his feet leave the ground. "Hey!" Xander rises into the air, grabbing at nothing with his hands, as though he can somehow pull himself back to earth.

"I'm going to kill you," growls Dallas. "I'll trap the demon in your dead body. It's the only way to save us all."

"Dallas! Stop! You could set the demon free." I jump to my feet and launch myself at him.

Dallas throws a hand in my direction, and I fly backward again and hit the wall. Xander starts spinning in mid-air, tumbling in the wind funnel Dallas has conjured. In the darkness I can't make out his face, but he's making a terrible choking noise. Dallas is sucking the air from his lungs.

I don't have much time. I have to use my magic. Last time I used it in the library, the building almost fell down. But what choice do I have? If I don't do it, Xander will die.

I search frantically for something sharp to cut myself with, and pull my house key out of my pocket. It takes all my strength to get the blunt end to rip through my skin, but when it does, my magic surges.

Flattening my bloody hand against the library's stone floor, I concentrate on an image of Dallas lying flat. From somewhere in the depths of my memory, I drag up a spell I learned years ago to send a tremor through rock, and mutter what I hope are the right words, trying to hold back my animal magic and just release my earth magic.

Strands of earth magic sink into the floor, and the ground ripples, toppling shelves and sending more books crashing to the ground. Dallas staggers, then falls against a bookshelf. The flashlight he dropped rolls further away, making it even harder to see.

Xander's still tumbling in mid air, but he's no longer making a choking noise. That's a bad sign. If he's not making any sound, it means he has no air left in his lungs.

My animal magic surges. Still entwined with my stone magic, it fights its way free from my slipping control and slams into something on the other side of the library.

An angry growl rumbles through the air like thunder, so loud it shakes the ground. The floor undulates again, then makes a loud cracking sound.

"Don't try to use your magic, stupid girl." Dallas pulls himself unsteadily to his feet on a floor that's still rippling. "You'll bring the whole building down and kill us all."

"Put Xander down and I'll stop." It's an empty promise. My magic has already been unleashed, and I have no idea what damage my animal magic might have done.

"Too late, Sapphira."

Fear clenches my heart. What does he mean, too late? Is Xander already dead?

No! I don't believe it. Xander can't be dead.

A deafening crash comes from the other side of the room. It sounds like something impossibly heavy has fallen over.

"You fool," hisses Dallas. "The building's collapsing."

Xander's body thumps to the ground, and with my heart in my mouth, I rush to him. "Xander? Are you okay?"

Dallas scuttles toward the door, but skids to a stop when another growl rumbles through the building. He slams his hand against a switch on the wall, and the room floods with light.

I squint in the sudden brightness, sinking down beside Xander. His face is deathly pale and his eyes are closed. I fumble for his pulse with my heart thumping, accidentally smearing the blood from the cut on my hand onto his neck.

"Give me more blood, or I'll rip you open and feast on your pain—"

I snatch back my hands as Jeqabeel's magic burns up my arms and its rasping voice fills my head. My whole body feels weak, like the demon stole some of my essence in the second I was touching him.

Xander drags in a gasping breath. His eyelids flutter, and I sag with relief. He's alive.

Dallas lets out a startled yelp, and I look up.

The stone gargoyle that guarded the library's entrance is crouched between the untoppled stacks, its small, thin tail swishing back and forth. It's now an enormous beast that looks a little like a dog, but with scales instead of fur. Its lips are pulled back in a snarl, displaying huge fangs that glisten with moisture. Its shoulders are taller than I am, and its jaws look big enough to swallow us whole.

So that's what happened to my magic.

Out of the corner of my eye, I spot Dallas creeping around the side of the stacks, toward the wall closest to the exit. He's moving slowly, obviously trying to avoid sudden movements that might attract the beast's attention.

"What happened?" asks Xander, his voice rough. He swallows hard, putting his hand to his neck. "My throat hurts."

The gargoyle takes a step toward us, its eyes focused on Xander. It growls again.

"Get up," I hiss quietly. "Don't move too quickly."

Xander lifts his head and stares at the creature. "What's that?"

"I accidentally brought the gargoyle to life." I hesitate. "More to life. Walking as well as talking."

"Can you stop it?"

I huff out a frustrated breath. "You mean make my magic do something useful? Unlikely."

A noise at the entrance to the library pulls my gaze away from the gargoyle. Dallas is standing at the bottom of the stairs that are the only exit from this level. He grins at me and waves one blood-covered hand. A shimmering barrier appears, blocking our way out. It looks like it's made from compressed air, so dense I doubt we'll be able to push our way through it.

Dallas has shut us in with the gargoyle, and Xander's still struggling to breathe, let alone get away from it.

The monster's head swings back to us. As it growls and starts toward us, I scramble to my feet and lurch away from Xander.

"Over here," I yell at it, edging toward an aisle where I'll have a clear path to run. "Good doggie. Do you remember me? I'm Saffy Black. You let me in here. Nice doggie."

It stares at me with cold gray eyes that seem to be the only part still made from stone, but at least it turns toward me instead of Xander. Its head lowers and it lets out a loud snort from its nostrils. Then it paws the ground like a bull about to charge.

I run.

Pounding down the middle of the aisle as fast as I can, I pump my arms hard. The ground shudders and the crash of heavy feet behind me tells me the beast is chasing me.

As soon as there's a break in the shelves, I dash into the gap, weaving as much as I can because the gargoyle is so big, it can't possibly be agile.

There's no way out, so I have no other plan other than drawing it away from Xander to give him a chance to recover.

The gargoyle crashes into shelves behind me, spilling

books. I don't dare to look around in case I trip, but it sounds like it's nipping at my heels.

"Saffy! Where are you?" Xander yells.

"I'm okay," I pant, turning a corner and racing down a new aisle.

Loud crashing behind me tells me the heavy gargoyle's taken the corner a little wide and demolished another stack of books. It's too close. It's gaining on me, and my lungs already feel like they're about to burst.

I need a new strategy.

Up ahead is one of those ladders the librarians use to get to the higher shelves. I sprint to it and scramble up, pulling myself onto the top of the tall shelving unit. Without stopping to see what the gargoyle's doing, I run across the top of the unit. It shakes underneath me, despite having being designed to hold hundreds of books.

When I reach the end of the unit, I risk a glance back. The gargoyle is nowhere in sight, and my chest expands with relief. Have I lost it?

Then I hear a flapping sound.

Something huge rises from between the stacks. *The gargoyle.* Its chunky wings flap too slowly, and it's way too heavy to fly. But I guess it's clueless about the laws of physics, because it's flying anyway.

Heart clenching, I stand still, panting and gaping at the creature as it lifts higher.

How is it doing that?

Then it snarls, and I spin back around and leap from my shelving unit onto the next one. The gargoyle flies after me, its wings making a whumph-whumph noise. Its heavy body hits the shelving unit, and I pinwheel my arms, fighting to keep my balance as the unit sways. The gargoyle hits it again, and I lose my footing on the swaying unit. I try to clutch the top of the shelves as I go over, but my fingers slip off it.

I hit the ground hard, and the air is knocked out of me. Books hit my body and thump to the ground all around me, and I curl into a foetal position, covering my head with my arms as the giant shelving unit topples. Screwing my eyes shut, I wait for it to land on me and squash me flat.

It doesn't.

I risk a glance through my arms and see the unit leaning over me, empty of books. It's balanced precariously against the shelves next to it, leaving me a small triangle of space.

I let out a breath.

I'm still alive.

It seems like a miracle. For a moment, I'm tempted to just lie still, sheltered by the stacks and the books that have fallen around me. Then I hear a growl and the light at one end of my protective triangle is blocked by the gargoyle's head. It reaches a paw through the opening, claws extended. Groping for me as though it's a cat and I'm a tasty mouse.

The shelving unit above me shudders and drops a little further toward me.

I have to get out of here.

But what can I do? The gargoyle won't stop, and I wouldn't stand a chance if I tried to fight such a big creature. It'll just keep coming for me until it kills me. Then it'll kill Xander too.

I crawl away from the gargoyle, over the fallen books, scrambling as fast as I can away from its reaching paw.

"Saffy!" Xander's shout comes from a short distance away. "Lead it to me."

He must have a plan.

I explode out from under the bookcase and sprint

toward his voice. Behind me the stacks shudder again, a loud crunching sound almost making me turn around to see what the gargoyle is doing. But I don't. I'm focused on Xander. I don't need to turn around. I just need to keep moving forward, to find Xander.

At first all I can hear is the pounding of my feet on the floor, and my panting breath as I try to push my panic down.

Then I hear the sound of heavy wings flapping behind me.

Don't look around.

I pump my arms, concentrating on running as fast as I can.

Don't look around.

Xander shouts again, and I power toward the sound.

Don't look around.

He's standing at the end of the row of shelves waving his arms up and down, as though trying to distract the gargoyle's attention. "Dive under there," he shouts, pointing at another toppled shelving unit that's only just being held off the floor by all the books underneath it. "I'll lead it away."

"Lead it where?" I pant.

"Trust me."

My lungs are about to burst, so I don't try to argue. I just dive under the fallen unit, shoving books aside as I scramble as far as I can into the tiny space.

"Here!" Xander yells. "Over here, you ugly mutt!"

A growl rips through the air, and my ragged breath catches in my throat.

Does Xander know the gargoyle can fly? What if his plan doesn't take that into account and the gargoyle catches him?

I wriggle back out from my hiding place and stand up.

The gargoyle is chasing Xander, its wings flapping as it runs. It's so close behind him its teeth are almost snapping into his back.

My stomach turns over as I realize where Xander's leading it. Ahead of him is a small reading room, only big enough to hold a table and four chairs. Xander's sprinting toward its open door, but there's no other way out of that room. He's going to get trapped in there.

Xander dives into the reading room with the gargoyle right behind him. It slams into the doorway of the small room, and tries frantically to pull its giant wings through the doorframe. I can imagine its enormous jaws snapping at Xander. The room's so tiny, he must be pressed against the far wall.

The gargoyle wedges one of its wings into the doorframe, but the other is still behind it, too big to squeeze through.

It's stuck. For now. But if the doorframe breaks, Xander's dead.

"Saffy!" His shout is muffled.

"I'm here." All I can see is the back of the gargoyle as it struggles to get in or out of the door.

"Use your magic. Reverse the spell and turn it back into stone."

His confidence leaves me breathless. He's seen first-hand the chaos my magic can unleash, yet he's trusting his life to the idea that I'm going to be able to fix this.

I nod to myself, dragging in a deep breath. I need to do this, and it has to work. I can't let Xander down.

Closing my eyes, I bring up the image of the gargoyle in my mind, remembering the way it used to be. Solid stone, fixed to one place. The gargoyle couldn't do more than talk.

When I have the picture so firmly in my mind that it

seems real, I dig into my hand with my ragged and broken fingernails, working at the cut I made earlier with my house key. I open the wound wider and force fresh blood out of my palm. It hurts like hell, but I ignore the pain, too focused on saving Xander to care. What little is left of my magic rises with the blood, and I gather it up, reaching deep inside myself to pull out every scrap.

I can't afford to mess this up.

I just wish I knew a spell for this. Something to help me direct and focus the magic. At least it's weaker now, instead of its usual explode-out-of-me strength, so maybe I have a chance of controlling it.

Stepping closer to the gargoyle, I press my bloody hand on its rump. Its tail flicks angrily from side to side, and it roars and squirms under my hand, trying to back out of the doorframe.

I ignore its struggles. All I can see now are the strands of magic that wrap around it. Animal magic glows brightly, each strand a fiery red. Snagged with it are strands of earth magic.

Carefully, panting with the effort, I feed new magic into it, using the new to break away the old. Both animal and earth magic at the same time, working together. The creature is both animal and stone, so both magics can flow to the same place for once. It helps a lot.

As each strand of magic breaks, the gargoyle's scales transform back into stone.

Its enormous wings go still and solid. Its body stiffens. The squirming stops.

"You did it, Saffy!" yells Xander.

A surge of jubilation and relief rushes through me, shattering my concentration. The last of my magic slips out of my grip. There's not much left, but it seeps into the gargoyle without me controlling or steering it.

The magic makes its tail grow longer. It swishes angrily from side to side, twice the size it was before and all too alive, even though the rest of the gargoyle is now solid stone.

The last strands of my magic arc up to the ceiling. Three overhead lights explode, and I duck as fragments of glass rain down.

When I straighten, I stand with my chest heaving, staring at the huge tail as it flicks back and forth. Most of the library's lights are still intact at least, so we haven't been plunged back into darkness.

In fact, nothing terrible happened this time. It's only the gargoyle's tail that didn't go to plan, so no real harm done. In fact, it looks kind of funny.

A maniacal chuckle bursts from my lips. Probably because I'm so relieved that the danger's past and right now, at least, I'm not staring down the barrel of our imminent and violent deaths.

A flicking tail can't kill me. That makes a pleasant change.

"Everything okay out there?" yells Xander.

"Peachy." Suppressing another chuckle, I take a step back to study the doorway to the reading room. The gargoyle's jammed into it so tightly, there's not so much as a crack to enable me to see past it.

"I just have one question," I shout. "How are you going to get out of that room?"

"Ah," says Xander. Then all I hear is a long, stumped silence.

Chapter Eight

Eventually, with the help of a broken piece of metal from one of the shelving units, we manage to splinter the wooden doorframe. Then it's a just matter of breaking the drywall around it, and pulling enough chunks out for Xander to squeeze his way out past the gargoyle.

Thankfully the gargoyle stays silent. I don't know whether it's lost its ability to make noises, or whether it's embarrassed about the whole event. Either way, I'm glad it doesn't speak. Whatever it might have had to say, I probably don't want to hear it.

Once Xander's safely out of the reading room, we finally get to look for the dark magic grimoire. The mess in the library makes it a lot harder to find, and I'm conscious of the clock ticking down the whole time we're searching through the collapsed stacks. The only good thing about how long it takes us is that by the time we've finally found my backpack with the grimoire inside, the wall of dense air Dallas left to block the library's exit has weakened. The spell's worn off enough for us to force our way through his barrier and into the stairwell.

After climbing the stairs, we limp outside. We're covered with drywall dust, and our clothes are filthy and torn. One of my hair elastics must have snapped because now my hair is only tied up on one side. Xander has a nasty cut down his arm where the gargoyle swiped him, and I have blood on my hand that I also managed to smear down my arm and onto both my T-shirt and jeans.

The guard on duty does a double-take, his eyes wide. "What the hell happened to you two?"

I blink at him, scratching my head like I have no idea what he's talking about. The scratching makes a cloud of drywall dust erupt from my hair. "What do you mean?" I ask blankly.

"We successfully catalogued the items." Xander's leaving a trail of dirty footprints behind him. "An important task, but a bit dull."

"Boring," I agree, using my filthy jeans to wipe the rest of the blood off my hand, before hitching up the backpack I've slung over my shoulder. I only hope the security guard doesn't remember that I didn't come in with a backpack.

We leave the guard gaping after us, and haul our aching bodies to where we parked the car. I get into the passenger seat, clutching the backpack on my lap. The grimoire's icy coldness seeps through the backpack's canvas, chilling my entire body.

"After all we went through to get that book, it better have the answers we need." Xander frowns at the road, weaving through the Baltimore traffic.

I slide the backpack into the foot well to stop the chill invading my body. "Is the demon still talking to you? What's it saying?" I instantly regret the question. "Scratch that. Forget I asked." I've heard its malevolent voice for myself.

He grimaces. "Believe me, you don't want to know what it's saying." He reaches to the stereo, but instead of playing his CD collection like he normally does, he turns on the radio. It blasts out an old Guns N' Roses song that isn't half bad, but for some strange reason, I almost wish he'd put on one of his usual CDs.

Not that his lame, old-man music could possibly be growing on me.

Xander grimaces. "This is almost as bad as the music you like." He lifts his hand again, hovering his finger over the stereo button. "Maybe I should switch it to Frank."

"Because listening to Frank Sinatra is better than listening to a foul demon who's trying to convince you to kill everyone you love?" I shrug, trying for the same joking tone as the last time we had this conversation. "Personally, I think it's a toss-up."

He shoots me a sideways look and drops his hand without switching it. "Maybe we should try playing that band you like. What's their name, the Fiery Buttplugs? Blast their music for long enough, and Jeqabeel might *want* to crawl back into its demon dimension."

"The Flaming Buttholes. And you're right. The demon's thousands of years old, so it makes total sense it would like your music better. Frank was probably cool when it was young."

He snorts. "Somebody should tell the Farting Buttboys that not even demons from hell like their music. I think that's the demographic they've been shooting for."

He grins at me and my heart clenches. This, right here, is exactly why I refuse to let anything happen to Xander. He has a terrifying demon inside him, and it's almost five o'clock which means he has about thirty-four hours left until the council turn him to stone, yet he can still joke with me.

I wish we were a normal mundane couple going home to do normal mundane things. Just for once I want to pretend we really could have that Netflix date Xander suggested. An ordinary night in front of the TV, and the only thing to worry about would be deciding what to watch.

"What kind of movies do you like?" I ask, tapping the song's beat on my leg.

He blinks at the change of subject, but says, "Cop shows. Crime dramas. Thrillers. That kind of thing."

"Really? Cop shows?" I screw up my face. "So you get home from a long day of being a cop, and to relax you watch cop shows?"

He shrugs. "I like them. Why? What do you watch?"

"My dad used to love reruns of shows from the eighties. Magnum P.I., Cheers, The A Team. So that's all I get on my television. Whatever spell he cast on it hasn't worn off yet."

Xander barks a laugh. "So when you and Jess sit down to watch something, you get to choose between Tom Selleck or Mr. T?"

"Thankfully, Jess isn't a big T.V. watcher, because I have no idea how I'd explain all the eighties reruns. It's been hard enough explaining the stray cats, not to mention Agnes the chicken." I grimace. "The giant dog statue in the courtyard might be the last straw."

He frowns. "Jess doesn't have any idea you can do magic? You haven't told her?"

"No way. Until Sylvia died a few weeks ago, I thought magic and witches were out of my life forever."

"Why? What happened?"

"The witch community wasn't exactly supportive after

my parents died. A lot of witches thought I killed them. They cut me off completely."

"So since then, you've been living without any magic at all?"

I nod slowly. "Except for my father's wards that protected the house, but they're gone now as well." I let out a sigh. "It took me a long time to learn how to live as a mundane, but I was doing it pretty successfully until Uncle Ray started killing people. Once this is over, I want my nice, normal mundane life back again." The thought is like a fairy-tale dream, hidden somewhere over the rainbow. In reality, I can't imagine how my life could ever go back to the way it was.

The song ends, and something even older comes on—a song by the Rolling Stones. Typical Xander, he probably has it tuned to a radio station that only plays old classics.

"You should tell Jess the truth," he says. "It's not fair to keep it from her."

"If I told her, it'd be like inviting magic back in to stay." I shake my head. "Besides, she wouldn't believe me. She'd think I'm crazy, like you did."

"You don't think your magic's back to stay?"

"Unfortunately, I think it is. If I could learn to control it properly, it wouldn't be such a problem. But like I say, I was doing okay with out it. And if I could get rid of it, I'd never need to deal with the council again." I let out a long breath, trying not to let myself dream about something that's unlikely to happen. The Rolling Stones song is called *You Can't Always Get What You Want*, like the radio's decided to rub it in.

Xander looks sympathetic. "For what it's worth, I still think you should tell Jess. If whatever happened to her today was caused by the Unseen, she deserves to know."

"But why would the Unseen go after Jess? What good would it do him?"

"Revenge for the snake? To force you to do what he wants?" Xander drums his fingers on the steering wheel. "He doesn't seem like the kind of person who needs much of an excuse. But if what happened has nothing to do with him, it's an awfully big coincidence. Something mysterious and terrible happens to your roommate just after you escape from a dark witch who's trying to manipulate you? I don't think so."

I swallow hard, turning to stare out of the window. If the Unseen is putting Jess in danger, I'm going to… I'm going to…

Huffing out a frustrated breath, I resist the urge to beat my fists against the dashboard. What can I do against the Unseen? His magic is stronger than mine. The only solution is to ask the council for help, which means going back to the people threatening Xander. The thought of asking them for favors turns my stomach.

As soon as Xander parks his car outside my house, I grab the backpack out of the foot well and head in to see Jess, anxious to make sure she's okay.

Mikey's on the living room couch, listening to music on his phone. He jumps up when he sees us. "What have you been up to?" He stares at my filthy clothes, then narrows his eyes at Xander. "What's going on?"

"Nothing," I tell him, glancing at the dirty footprints I'm leaving on the floor. "We just got caught up in some dirt. Is Jess awake?"

Mikey stares at me with confusion in his eyes. His mouth opens slowly, as though he's trying to decide which questions to ask first. His eyes flick from me to Xander and back again. "Caught up in dirt?" he mutters. Then he presses his lips together and gives his head a shake. "She's still snoring," he says. "I've been checking on her every ten minutes."

"Thanks for staying." I'm grateful he's decided not to press me for answers, though judging by his expression, he's decided Xander and I were doing something kinky.

"Nobody showed up here while we were out?" asks Xander.

"Nope. Were you expecting someone?"

"Not exactly." Xander waves a dismissive hand. "You can take off now."

"We'll call you when she wakes up," I add, because the two men seem determined to rub each other the wrong way. Too much testosterone in a small space, I guess.

Mikey hesitates, scrubbing a hand over his unshaven chin so hard, I hear his whiskers rasp against his palm. "I don't want to leave her." He blows out his breath. "But I've skipped work so often, they'll can me if I don't turn up."

"Go." I clap him on the back, then steer him toward the door. "I'll take care of her."

He makes me promise to call him with an update on her condition before I shut the door behind him. Then I turn to Xander and hold up the backpack. "Come on. We can look at the grimoire upstairs."

On the way past Jess's bedroom, I peek in at her. Sure enough, she's still curled up in bed.

"She okay?" murmurs Xander from behind me.

I nod and motion him through to my parents' old bedroom. The walls of this room are covered with the information I collected when I was trying to figure out who killed them. I shut the door behind us before sliding the dark magic grimoire out of the backpack and onto the large desk that now takes pride of place in the center of the room.

The grimoire's cover is so black, it looks like it's sucking in all traces of light from around it and devouring everything good. Just looking at it makes me uneasy.

"All I can think about is how its pages licked the Unseen's fingers." Xander shudders.

He's standing a short distance from the book, and I step back too. I'll have to work myself up to touching it.

"The Unseen was giving it blood," I say. "And it probably wasn't his own blood."

"Does that make a difference?"

I nod. "Witches use their own blood to cast spells. But *dark* witches extract other peoples' blood, and the more pain and suffering they cause in the process, the more potent the blood is, and the stronger the magic."

"Are there many dark witches?"

"Only the Unseen, as far as I know. Dark magic is forbidden by the council. It's supposed to be more powerful than ordinary magic, but using it corrupts a witch's mind and sends them mad."

Xander nods. "I noticed the Unseen's sanity spell-book had some pages missing. But if he uses dark magic, why doesn't the council arrest him?"

"Arrest him?" I snort. "The council doesn't arrest people. They turn them into stone statues." I bite my tongue, because I probably shouldn't have reminded him about the council's favorite quirk. Pretty soon the sun will be setting. A whole day almost gone, and all our hopes hinge on the grimoire having something in it that will help.

His gaze flicks to the softening light outside the window, as though he's thinking the same thing I am. "I wouldn't mind seeing the Unseen turned into a statue."

"He's managed to avoid it by staying under the radar. I don't think they realized what he was doing. But now I've seen it firsthand, I'll tell the council."

The Unseen's bowl of blood on his spell table comes to

mind, and I wonder where the blood came from. Was it some innocent mundane he cast a spell over? Could it have been another witch's blood?

There's no way to find out, and I don't have time to stand here wondering. I have to get the demon out of Xander. The Unseen can wait.

I drag in a deep breath, clenching and unclenching my fingers. Then I step forward, lift the grimoire's icy cover, and flip the book open.

Its pages swirl with black mist, and it feels creepily like there's something hiding below the surface that's waiting to leap out. The pages rise and fall softly, like the book is breathing.

My magic surges inside me, reacting to the open grimoire. Not in a good way. It feels like it's trying to explode out of me.

"Can you read it?" asks Xander. "The pages look black to me."

I shake my head. "It's hiding its spells because it wants blood."

"Should we give it some of mine?" He offers his hand.

"It'd be dangerous to let it have any." I swallow, all too aware that we may have no choice. "Powerful old grimoires like this one can sometimes cast their own spells. The person who wrote it put his own blood into it, and the power can grow—"

A muffled ringing sound makes me jump. The phone handset in my bedroom is ringing. "Wait here," I tell Xander. "Don't do anything." I dash out of the room, rushing to answer the phone before it wakes Jess. I really need to get a new cellphone.

"Hello?"

"Sapphira, It's Magnus. Have you made any progress

learning how to transfer the demon into a different receptacle?"

I hesitate, thinking of the grimoire. "No," I say shortly.

"The Veritas had a vision of disaster. I don't think we can give you much more time."

My heart stutters. "What? But you gave me forty-eight hours. You can't cut it short."

"We can't take the chance that the demon might get free." Magnus sounds weary. "This is far bigger than one person. We're putting the entire population at risk."

"Give me more time. I need more time," I say desperately.

"I'm afraid we can't afford to—"

I hang up before he can say any more, unable to bear hearing him pronounce Xander's sentence. I feel sick and shaky and I'm afraid I might vomit.

Slowly, I walk back to my parent's bedroom, where Xander and the grimoire are waiting. Once there, I drag in a deep breath and make my mind up. Giving in to its dark magic is our only chance now.

"Stand back," I tell Xander.

On the desk next to the grimoire is my mother's ceremonial knife. I grab it and run the blade over my ring finger, hissing when the sting hits. Blood swells from the cut.

My magic surges, the strands of animal and earth magic fighting to get free.

This can't be good. The more I use my magic, the faster I seem to recover. In spite of exhausting it in the library, it already feels chaotic and powerful again. It takes all my strength to hold it inside me.

This is too dangerous. Why am I giving the grimoire what it wants? There must be another way.

I drop the knife on the table and pull my hand back, grabbing my cut finger to stop the bleeding.

Too late.

A drop of blood lands on the grimoire's open page.

For a second, it's like the world stands still. I freeze, waiting for whatever gruesome thing the book is going to throw at me.

Then the grimoire's pages rise up, reaching for my hand. As they get close, they pull my magic free, yanking it out of me. Writhing tendrils of magic pour from my fingers as the book pulls both my animal and earth magic into itself. I cry out, but I can't move my hand away.

The black mist clears away from the book's pages, exposing the words and runes written in blood that roil and tremble underneath. The book's spells are finally exposed, and a surge of hope goes through me as I stare down at the words.

Finally, I can find the answers we need.

Then I feel the book changing my magic, corrupting it and turning it into something that feels dark and evil. My vibrant, electric strands of magic go black.

The dark strands of magic reach out toward Xander. No, not Xander. To the demon inside him. The grimoire was created by Jeqabeel's disciple, and now it's reaching out to its master, using my magic to strengthen the demon.

I can't let that happen.

Frantically, I pull the magic back to myself, fighting to yank it free, like a magical tug-of-war.

"Get out of here, Xander," I scream. "Go!"

As he stumbles backward toward the door, the frustrated magic builds above the grimoire, amplified by its dark power, but unable to settle inside its pages or find its demon target. It rushes around me in a tornado, lifting my hair and filling my ears with its roar.

Sparks of energy flash like lightning.

The magic builds until I can't bear it any more. My body feels like it's being turned inside out, pulled in every direction, my arms forced wide by a pressure I don't understand. I want to open my mouth, to let out a scream, anything, to release the pressure, but I'm locked in place, unable to do anything.

Energy surges flash out of the grimoire, and it shudders violently. Its pages flip frantically back and forth, moving too fast to read.

And then the pages stop turning and lie flat. A huge rune fills the spread. It pulses blood red. Black calligraphy writhes around the rune, but I can't make out what it says. The grimoire expands, as if the magic inside it is too big to be contained in its pages.

The grimoire is using my magic, controlling it to get what it wants. But it's *my* magic. Somehow, I have to turn the power against it.

I reach both arms out, as though I can grab hold of the magic. Concentrating hard, I can see the strands that are still glowing, a chaotic mess of magic swirling inside the grimoire's dark tornado. I fight to take hold of them again, to yank them away from the grimoire and drag back them into myself. The strands burn cold as though they've been charged with the book's icy darkness. The cold seeps inside me, and pain shoots through my body. I grind my teeth, forcing myself to keep hold of the magic. Fighting against the power of the grimoire.

The blood is freezing in my veins and my skin is turning black. Every cell in my body screams with pain. But I'm doing it. I'm pulling my magic away from the grimoire. I'm taking control—

The grimoire explodes.

The shockwave throws me backward and I smack hard against the wall.

Ash rains down on me and I cover my face with my arms. My face feels singed by the force of the explosion and my ears are ringing.

When I slowly drop my arms and lift my head, I don't recognise the room. Everything is covered in a thick layer of black ash.

My head jerks toward the door. "Xander?" Then I cough as ash fills my throat.

He steps forward, blinking. He's covered in ash too. "You okay?"

I stand slowly, trying not to breathe in any more black powder.

Incredibly, the grimoire is still on the desk, lying open. Maybe its spells are still readable and we can still use it to banish the demon.

I reach out to brush the ash from its pages. As soon as my fingers touch it, a cloud of black smoke erupts, and the book collapses into nothing.

The grimoire, our only hope of finding a way to save Xander, is gone.

Chapter Nine

"Saffy? Are you okay?" Jess's voice comes from outside the closed door. "What was that noise?"

I stiffen and stare at Xander. She's never seen inside this room. I told her I was keeping it locked because it still had my parents' belongings inside, and I wanted to preserve their memory.

"I'm okay," I call back. "It was nothing."

"I really think you should tell her the truth," murmurs Xander.

I stare at him for a moment, then give a reluctant nod. He's right. I can't keep hiding my magic from her.

Xander opens the door. "Hey," he says. "Don't freak out over the mess. I'll let Saffy tell you all about it while I get the vacuum cleaner. You keep it in the laundry room, right?"

I nod. He heads toward the stairs, and Jess stares at me, her eyes wide. She's in her pyjamas, her long blonde hair still tangled from sleep. She looks a lot better than when I put her to bed a few hours ago, and some color has come back to her cheeks.

"How are you feeling?" I ask. "Do you remember what happened to you?"

She steps closer, staring into the room. "Why are you covered in ash?" She ignores my questions. "What happened in there? It looks like a bomb went off. Literally."

Looking around, I nod my agreement. It does look like the scene of a major disaster. The floors and walls are covered with ash, and the papers I'd pinned to the walls—the information I'd collected over years of wondering about my parent's deaths—are so black they're unreadable.

"Jess…" I hesitate. This is even harder to say than I expected. "There's something I've been hiding from you. But now I have to tell you." The words come out in a rush, and I watch her face closely to see how she reacts. But all I see is concern.

"Tell me what? Are you in trouble?"

I take a deep breath, trying not to cough when I suck in more ash. I can't believe I'm doing this. She's my best friend, and admitting the truth is going to change everything. I need her in my life, and if she freaks out, she might leave. The idea makes me feel desperate. Am I doing the right thing?

"The truth is, I'm in all kinds of trouble," I admit. "I'll tell you everything, and you're going to think I'm insane, but I promise, I'm not." I wipe my black, ash-covered hands on my black, ash-covered jeans and walk toward the door. "How about I go and clean up first? Then we can sit down and talk."

Jess crosses her arms, standing in the doorway so I can't get past. "Tell me now."

"But I should really take a shower and—"

"Now, Saff."

I nod, accepting that I can't delay this a second longer.

This is it.

"I'm a witch," I say in a rush. "My family were all witches. My magic got messed up when my parents died, so I haven't been able to use it. Now it's free again, and I can use it, but I can't control it. And Xander's been hurt because of me." The words come tumbling out in an unstoppable rush. "He's been possessed by a jackal-headed demon, and the Blood Council wants to turn him to stone, to try and contain the demon. I don't know how much more time they're going to give us, but I'm pretty sure it's not going to be long enough for me to figure out how to get the demon out of him. There's also a dark witch after me, and I'm afraid that whatever happened to you might be connected. Which would mean it's my fault you were hurt."

I run out of air and take another breath. Jess's eyes are wide. I can't tell what she's thinking. I wait for her to say something but she just stares at me.

"It sounds crazy," I say. "Believe me, I know it does. But I need you to keep an open mind."

"Why are you telling me this?" She sounds dumbstruck.

"Because you're my friend and I don't want to lie to you anymore. Things are getting too dangerous around here and I can't keep you in the dark." I step forward, wanting to put my hand on her arm. Only I'm still covered in black ash, so I don't. "Say something, Jess."

She draws in a loud breath. "You've been keeping secrets. But so have I. There's something you don't know—"

A bang comes from downstairs. Was that the front door? Xander went down to get the vacuum cleaner. What if Magnus has turned up to take him back to the council chambers so they can turn him to stone?

"Sorry." I push past Jess. "We'll talk more in a minute, okay? I just need to check on Xander."

I race down the stairs and into the living room. Then I freeze.

Xander is sitting on the couch and the Unseen is hunched over him. With his back to me, the bones of his spine are showing through the Unseen's baggy clothes. He's as thin as a cadaver.

I open my mouth to shout at the Unseen to get away from Xander. Then I catch sight of Xander's face and my voice dies in my throat. His pupils are blood red.

"I will give you the power you desire." Xander stares up at the Unseen. "Once I've feasted on blood." I can see Xander's the one who's speaking, only the voice coming out of him is a slow, contemptuous drawl that doesn't sound like him at all. It sends a horrible chill down my back.

The voice belongs to Jeqabeel.

The Unseen has his hands on Xander's shoulders, and there's blood smeared on Xander's ash-covered clothes. Tendrils of magic cover the Unseen's hands and Xander's shoulders. I don't know how the Unseen did it, but he must have cast a spell to help the demon take control of Xander's body.

"Find a way to rid me of this cursed mundane," the demon inside Xander orders. "It has no power. I may as well be inside a slab of dead meat."

The Unseen nods. "You can count on me, my lord. I won't fail you."

My heart is thumping hard, and my hands start to tremble.

Is this the vision the Veritas saw? The Unseen strengthening Jeqabeel with his dark magic, helping the demon use Xander as its puppet? What's this doing to

Xander? Is he still in there or is demon destroying his mind?

I have to stop this. But how?

I step forward, already slicing my fingernail into the cut on my hand to start fresh blood flowing. But the grimoire pulled what was left of my magic out, depleting it. Besides, with so little control over my magic, I'm no match for the Unseen.

Maybe I can overpower him if I catch him by surprise.

I take another soft step toward him, and the Unseen jerks around and stares at me. So much for taking him by surprise.

"Hello Sapphira." An unpleasant smile crawls over the Unseen's face, showing off his sharpened teeth.

"Get away from Xander," I snap.

"You can't give me orders, broken witch." He drags his gaze down my body and up again, probably wondering why I'm covered in black ash. Then he flicks his bloody hand at me, and I feel a jolt of connection run through my body. He still has my mother's ring, which means he can force me to do whatever he wants.

"Let Xander go, or else." I plant my feet and glower at him, trying to sound threatening. It's an empty bluff and I'm sure he knows it.

He smirks. "Or else what?"

Behind him on the wall is a portrait of my mother and father, looking down in a loving way, their faces frozen in time. If they were really here, they'd have the power to banish the Unseen. In fact, he probably wouldn't have gotten through the door in the first place. But me? I'm helpless against him. One of his hands is still on Xander's shoulder, and Xander's pupils are glowing red, the demon still in control.

"What's going on?" Jess's voice comes from behind me,

and my heart stops beating. This is bad enough without putting her in danger too.

"Go back upstairs, Jess," I say without turning around.

"Why?" Her footsteps tell me she's most of the way down the staircase. "Who's that man, Saffy? And what's wrong with the detective?"

"Jess, please. Get out of here."

The Unseen moves his creepy smile to her. "Another pretty one," he says. "Come closer. Let me take a look at you."

Xander makes a horrible growling sound that chills me to my core. "Kill them both."

"Of course, my lord." The Unseen motions me closer with his blood-covered hand. A red tendril extends from his palm, snaking toward my chest. When it reaches me, my feet move of their own accord. Unable to stop myself, I walk toward him until I'm standing right in front of him. If only I could lift my hand, I could tear my mother's necklace from around his neck. But I can't do anything except stand still with my teeth clenched and every muscle straining, trying to fight against his power.

"Stop it," shouts Jess, jumping the last of the stairs.

Xander lets out another blood-chilling growl, his red eyes fixed on me. "Kill the witch," he hisses.

The Unseen grabs me by the neck with his free hand. His hot breath gusts over my face as he squeezes. His fingers dig painfully into my throat. I fight to drag in air, but I can't breathe. I can't do anything but stand silent and motionless, utterly helpless though my whole body is screaming for oxygen. He's going to choke me to death and I can't even move a finger to stop him.

"Get away from her." Jess's voice rises. "Let her go!"

The Unseen lifts his other hand from Xander's shoulder. I can't see what happens, but Jess lets out a loud cry, like he hurt her.

"Get back," he orders.

Instead of obeying, Jess launches herself at the Unseen, blood dripping from a deep cut across her face. She grabs the Unseen's arms, ripping his hand from my neck. They stagger backward together.

With a flash of light, the Unseen and Jess vanish into thin air.

Chapter Ten

I stare dumbfounded at the empty space where the Unseen and Jess were just a moment ago. Where'd they go? In all the time I spent around witches when I was growing up, I've never seen anyone vanish like that. I had no idea it was possible.

The Unseen is even more powerful than I realized.

Xander makes a strangled sound and I turn to him, my heart thumping. His eyes are almost blue again, but there's a faint hint of red around their edges. Is he in control, or is the demon?

"Xander." I move toward him, but manage to stop myself before I take hold of his arm. "Are you in control again? Are you okay?"

"It's me." He reaches up with one shaking hand and rubs his palm over his face. "The demon's loud now, though. I don't know if I can…" He shakes his head. "Saffy, you'd better lock me up. Do you have a room with a lock on the door?"

"If I do that…" I break off. I was going to say that if I lock him up, our chances of finding a way to get Jeqabeel out of his body sink even lower. But with the grimoire gone, I have no idea where we go from here anyway. I'm out of ideas.

"We have to find Jess," I say instead. "The Unseen took her, and we need to get her back."

"Whatever you do, you'll have to do it without me." His shoulders slump. "I can't be trusted."

I shake my head, unwilling to shut Xander away. "I don't have a room that locks from the outside."

"Then get some rope and tie my hands and feet."

"No, I can't do that to you. Besides, you're okay now, right? We don't need to—"

"Saffy." He stands up and runs his hand through his hair the way he does when he's frustrated. "I don't know what the Unseen did, but the demon's a lot stronger than it was. I'm in control right now, but I don't know how long I can keep it that way." He steps closer, giving me a grim look that makes my chest tighten. "I need to know you're safe. If the demon takes control, it might try to hurt you, and I can't live with that." His hands lift as though he wants to take my upper arms, then he lowers them again and huffs out a loud breath. "This sucks. But please, do what I ask."

"Okay." I try not to let the despair I feel show on my face. "There's some rope in my truck."

I head outside for the rope and come back to find Xander sitting on one of the dining room chairs. Crouching in front of him, I bind first his feet, then his wrists. I'm careful not to touch him as I tie the knots.

"What happened to Jess?" he asks, as I loop some rope around his upper body, tying his arms and torso to the chair. "How'd she disappear like that?"

"The Unseen took her away somehow. But I don't know why he'd do that when the demon had just ordered him to kill us both. He seemed like he wanted to obey Jeqabeel, then he vanished into thin air. It doesn't make sense." I pull the knots tight around his body, trying not to let my fear for Jess take over. What could the Unseen want with her?

A shudder runs through Xander, and I glance up in alarm. "Xander? Did I tie the rope too tightly?"

His pupils glow red.

I scramble backward, scooting away from him as fast as I can. Seeing the demon staring out of Xander's face is the most god-awful thing I could have imagined.

Xander holds up his bound hands and speaks coldly in the demon's slow drawl. "You think rope will contain me? I'm the most powerful demon to ever walk your earth."

"Stop it," I growl even though I know I'm wasting my breath. "Leave Xander alone."

"This pathetic human?" Xander's face distorts into a furious grimace. "I'll bathe in his worthless blood." Bending his head, he manages to lift Xander's bound hands close enough to his mouth to bite viciously at Xander's thumb, tearing away a chunk of flesh with his teeth. Blood spurts from the wound.

Bile rises and I barely keep from gagging. "Stop it!" I grab the trailing end of the rope around his wrists and yank his hands down. It takes all my strength to tie them to the chair while he struggles to get free, fighting my every move.

When I have his hands secure, I grab a cushion from the couch, rip off its cover and stuff the fabric into Xander's mouth. At least now he can't bite anything, but I need a proper gag so he doesn't just spit it out. I'd better get something to bind the wound as well. There's a lot of blood. Enough to make my magic thrum inside my veins.

While I run to grab a first aid kit, Xander spits the

fabric from his mouth and shouts curses at me, promising to kill me in a number of inventive ways.

I come back to find that he's tipped the chair over, and is on the floor with blood smeared all over him. He's worked the sleeve of his T-shirt up far enough to tear another chunk out of his own flesh, this time from his shoulder.

"Stop." Tears prickle, but I refuse to let them out. Xander will subdue the demon and regain control. I know he will. I just need to give him time.

Moving behind him, I manage to heave both him and the chair back upright. Then I fashion a gag out of a cut piece of fabric and a long bandage. Just as I'm tying it, somebody pounds on the door.

I freeze.

Who could be knocking? Not the Unseen, he'd use a spell to unlock the door.

Could it be Jess, escaped from the Unseen? Last I saw her, she was in her pyjamas so she definitely wouldn't have her house key on her. I start toward the door, then hesitate. What if it's Magnus and the other council members, here to take Xander away?

While I'm trying to make up my mind what to do, whoever it is pounds against the door even harder.

Leaving Xander in the living room, I go to the door. Times like this, I wish I had one of those peepholes to look out and see who's there. But I don't. So I drag in a deep breath and open it.

Five men in police uniforms stand on my front porch. The policemen have their hands on their guns.

One of them steps forward. "Sapphira Black?" he demands. He's got freckles on his cheeks, and a nose so large, it overshadows the rest of his face.

I'm so shocked that I nod. What are the police doing here?

Then I remember. Xander and I were arrested and managed to escape from police custody. We're wanted criminals. Fugitives from justice. It's a sign of how messed up everything is that I'd pushed all that to the back of my mind.

I don't know what to do. Try to reason with them? Run? This is the last thing I was expecting.

The policeman looks me up and down, his eyes narrowed. He's probably wondering why I'm covered with black ash and blood.

"Sapphira Black, you're under arrest for murder, conspiracy to commit murder, evading arrest and kidnapping." The policeman keeps speaking, but I don't hear the words. All I can do is stare at his enormous nose, my heart thumping. I don't have time for this.

They're still investigating Sylvia's death, but that seems like it happened a long time ago, in another life. The case has been solved, I know who killed her and why. Problem is, there's no way the police would believe a story about my uncle being possessed by a demon.

Could I use my magic to send the police away? If I try, anything could happen. I could accidentally kill these men. Besides, they might be able to help me find Jess.

"My roommate is missing," I tell them. "Her name is—"

"Where is he? Does she have Xander here?" A high-pitched woman's voice comes from behind the group, and she pushes her way through.

Xander's mother. The Mayor of Baltimore. She's wearing a severe black suit and an even more severe glare. When she narrows her eyes at me, her expression's almost as chilling as the demon's was.

One of the policemen steps forward with a pair of handcuffs. He grabs one of my wrists, then the other, fastening the handcuffs on while I stare down in shock.

This is the last thing I need.

"We have a warrant to search your premises," says the policeman with the nose, holding up a sheet of paper. "We have reason to believe you're holding Xander Trent against his will."

The rest of the officers stride past me into the house. If my heart could sink any lower, it'd be in my shoes. I can't believe this is happening.

"Step this way, Ms. Black." Sergeant Nose takes hold of my arm, drawing me away from my front door. "If you could stay outside too please, Mayor, until we've checked the house."

"My son might be in there," snaps Xander's mother.

"Yes, ma'am. But we can't risk contaminating a crime scene."

"You don't understand," I say desperately. "None of this is how it looks. You need to let me go or Xander's going to die, and my roommate—"

"He's in here," shouts one of the officers from inside the house. "And he's injured."

The mayor's eyes widen. Before the detective can stop her, she bolts inside.

Sergeant Nose curses loudly, then grabs my arm and tows me into the living room.

Xander is lying on the floor, still tied to the chair. His pupils are red, and his arms and face are covered with blood. One of the policemen must have pulled the gag out of his mouth.

"Oh my dear lord," gasps Xander's mother. "What has she done?"

Xander stares up at her, unblinking. "Untie me," he orders in the demon's cold drawl.

His mother crouches and fumbles with the ropes that bind him to the chair, loosening the one around his arms so he can yank his bound wrists up.

"Ma'am." One of the policeman takes her arm and tugs her back up to her feet. "Let us do that, please, Mayor Trent. You need to wait outside."

She jerks her arm away from him, making no move to leave. Sergeant Nose crouches to keep untying Xander. The other three are nowhere to be seen.

My breath catches in my throat and I try to swallow down the huge lump that's stuck there. They're going to set Xander free, and who knows what hideous things he'll do? He could tear more chunks from his flesh and kill himself. Or he could kill them.

I have to stop them from untying him. The only way to do that is to get the demon to show its true nature.

"You're weak, Jeqabeel," I yell at Xander. "You think you're so evil? I've eaten sandwiches that were scarier than you."

He snarls at me, an animal sound. "Speak again and I'll kill you, witch." His voice is low and guttural, and he sounds more animal than human.

Sergeant Nose has already untied the rope that was securing Xander's torso to the chair. Now he draws back, his expression shocked.

His mother is pale. "Xander? Darling, what did she do to you?"

Xander spits out a giant gob of blood. "This human is dead flesh. Its blood is worthless. I need *power*." His eyes glitter with malevolence. "Kill this human. I order you to do it now!"

His mother swings around to glare at me. "Xander's been drugged. That girl must have drugged my son."

"What did he take?" the policeman asks me. "How long has he been like this?"

"It's not drugs." I raise my voice. "It's a lame-ass demon. And if ugly were a crime, it would be the one in handcuffs."

Xander snarls, jerking his tied wrists around, struggling to get free. "I'll rip your heart out and grind your bones into powder."

"What drugs did you give him?" Xander's mother demands, glaring at me.

"We'll do the full spectrum of drug tests on them both at the station," Nose assures her.

I chew my lip. How long do we have before Magnus comes for Xander? Should I go quietly with the police? Or is there some way I could get us out of here?

His mother crouches in front of Xander, and before the policeman can stop her, she pulls the rope free from his wrists. Xander reacts immediately, locking his hands around her throat. His eyes glow brighter as he squeezes, and he lets out a gleeful laugh.

Both policemen wrestle with Xander and manage to break his grip. Gasping, Mayor Trent falls backward, pulling herself as far away from Xander as she can get. Her face is pale, and her neck is already bruising. At least she's not showing any sign of hearing the demon talk inside her head like it does when I touch Xander. That would really shock her.

Xander struggles with the policemen, then leans in to bury his teeth in one man's ear. The policeman howls and Sergeant Nose leaps to his rescue, handcuffing Xander's hands behind his back and holding him down. The policeman stumbles back with his hands pressed to the side of his head. "He bit me!"

Xander laughs again. His lips are pulled back and his teeth are red with blood. His wild red eyes glitter. He looks like he's enjoying himself.

I'd hoped Jeqabeel would show what it really is, but it's still shocking. The demon's putting on a show for its audience.

Sergeant Nose checks the handcuffs are secure around Xander's wrists, then straightens, looking stunned. "I've been in the force a long time, but I've never seen anything like this." His brows draw down and his expression darkens as he turns to me. "What the hell did you do to him?"

I shake my head. "I didn't do anything."

"This is her fault." His mother lunges at me as if she's about to attack me, and the sergeant moves in front of me.

"Mayor Trent, we need you to remain calm." He steps closer to her, using his bulk to make her take a step back. "Please allow us to do our jobs."

The mayor takes a deep breath, and then another, calming herself with a visible effort. "I want you to promise me that she's going to rot in jail for doing this to my son."

"We'll do our best, ma'am," says Sergeant Nose. He looks at his bitten colleague. "Parker, get an ambulance here, and notify the medics their patient is violent. You'll also need to get that bite checked." He raises his voice, calling into the hallway. "Have we finished searching the premises?"

A third policeman joins us, coming into the living room from the hallway. "Just waiting on the men upstairs, sir. They're checking the second floor."

"Sir," calls a muffled voice from the top of the stairs. "You'll want to take a look at this."

"Take her to the station." Nose hands me over to the

third officer, then heads up the stairs. I already know what he's going to see. My parents' bedroom, covered in a thick layer of black ash. They'll probably accuse me of running a meth lab. Or perhaps they'll be able to clean the soot off the research that was covering the walls, and it'll convince them I'm a serial killer, planning my kills before tearing out the hearts of my victims.

Whatever way they look at it, I'm screwed.

"Wait," I shout at Nose's back. "My roommate's missing. You need to find her."

He stops half way up the stairs, and turns. "Missing?" He sounds suspicious.

"Jess Tremaine. She's my age and my height, with blonde hair and blue eyes. She's in danger."

He starts back down the stairs toward me, tugging a notebook out of his breast pocket. "What kind of danger?"

I hesitate, trying to come up with an answer. Sending the police to the Unseen's house would be useless. They'd just see an innocent old man in a sweet, fairy-tale house. Hiding in plain sight is what he's best at. Not to mention that going there would put them in danger, seeing as the dark witch needs other people's blood for his magic.

Maybe reporting her missing isn't the best idea after all, but I have to do *something*. How can I rescue Jess if I'm in custody?

"When did you last see your roommate?" Sergeant Nose's pen hovers over his notepad, and there's a note of impatience in his voice.

"Earlier today," I admit. "But I have good reason to believe she's in serious trouble."

"What reason?" His eyes narrow. "Did she take the same drugs you did?"

"I told you, I didn't take any drugs."

"Did you hurt her?"

"Me? No! Of course not."

Nose shoves his notebook back in his pocket and looks at one of the other policeman. "Put out an alert for the roommate. I want her brought in." Then his narrow-eyed gaze goes back to me. "You can tell me all about it at the station."

Two policemen take me outside and push me into a cop car. I sit in the back seat, my handcuffed hands heavy in my lap, and my brain spinning. Who knows where they're going to take Xander. After the performance Jeqabeel put on, he'll probably end up in a psychiatric ward.

Time is ticking away, and my chances of being able to figure out a way to save Xander are slipping away. I won't be able to do a thing locked up in a police cell while he's taken who-knows-where.

I close my eyes, taking a deep breath and trying to remain calm. But how can I when Jess is missing and Xander's as good as dead?

Chapter Eleven

"You'll remain here until you've had a blood test."
The young police officer removes my handcuffs, and I rub my sore wrists with relief. "We need to find out what drugs you took." Despite his hard words, his hands are gentle, and he isn't scowling at me. He ushers me into a holding cell with a bare mattress for a bed, and a lidless metal toilet.

"I'm not on any drugs," I insist. "If you've got questions, you need to ask me now. I don't have time to wait. Both my roommate and Xander are in serious danger."

"A medic will be here in a minute to get a blood sample."

"I didn't take anything," I say for the millionth time, grabbing his arm to stop him leaving. "Please, you don't understand. I have to get out of here."

He pulls away. "Wait for the medic. You'll get a chance to tell your story soon."

The cell door slams, and I'm alone in the brightly lit room. I pace to the bed but don't sit down. What the hell am I going to do? My only option is to use magic to get out of here, but even if it works, what then? How will I find Xander?

The policeman comes back, and this time he's with a middle-aged medic who pushes a medical tray on wheels into the room.

"Sit down on your bed and hold out your arm," says the medic. His bored demeanour tells me he's not interested in chit-chat.

"I don't want you to draw my blood." I don't know how my magic will react to a whole vial of blood being taken, but I doubt I'll be able to control it.

"Court order says you have to give us a sample." The policeman folds his arms. "Either let him do it the easy way, or we'll have to do it the hard way."

Letting out a frustrated breath, I sit down. My vein stands out in the crook of my elbow, bulging a little as though my blood is eager for release. This isn't going to be fun.

I try one more time. "I don't think—"

But it's too late. I feel the sting as the medic pushes the needle in. I tense. My magic is already fighting to be free.

I can either try to contain it, or I can let it go, and maybe use it to get out of here. I need the cell to open, and for the policeman and medic to be unable to stop me leaving.

Focus. I need to focus.

"That's it," says the medic, as my blood starts to flow. "Just relax."

The vial fills, my blood bright red. There's a lot of it. So much, I don't have a chance to hold my magic in. It swells, chaotic and violent, pouring out with my blood.

My control slips.

I grab hold of the image of what I want to happen,

concentrating on an image of the cell door swinging open and the men inside the cell falling asleep.

The magic tears out of me with so much force, it punches the air from my lungs. My animal magic pours into the policeman and the medic, and they slump to the ground.

Then my earth magic slams into the cell door with the force of a bomb, blowing it into a million shards. I duck, covering my head as the shards fly at me, each one a sharp missile capable of slicing through flesh and bone.

I keep my head down, flinching as flying bits of metal crash around me. I'm certain one's going to decapitate me, but not a single piece hits my body.

When the room finally falls silent, I lift my head and gape at the devastation.

The cell door is now a gaping hole, open to the hallway outside. Chunks of the door have torn through the walls, carving large holes. There's debris everywhere and the air is thick with dust.

The policeman and medic are both lying on the ground near my feet. The policeman has a metal shard sticking out of one arm. The medic has blood on his white lab coat.

They both lie motionless, and I crouch over them. Running my hands over the neck of first the policeman, then the medic, I hunt desperately for a pulse. Shouldn't I be able to feel their hearts beating?

I grab their wrists, frantically searching for the faintest flutter, then press my ear against each of their chests. I don't know if it's because my own heart is pounding so loudly in my ears, but if either of them is still alive, I can't tell.

What if I've killed them?

I moan quietly. This is a nightmare. If I've killed two innocent people, I'll never forgive myself.

I take hold of the metal shard in the policeman's arm, wondering if I should pull it out. But if he's still alive, doing that could make him bleed to death. Better to leave it where it is.

The blood on the medic's coat is mostly from a deep gash in the back of his shoulder. The medical tray he brought in with him has fallen over and its contents are strewn across the floor, but I search through the debris and find a bandage to cover the wound. Is it a good sign that the medic's still bleeding? One thing I do know is that both men need medical help right away.

Struggling to my feet, I move to the blown-out cell door and peer down the short, empty hallway. There are two other empty cells on one side of the passage, and a closed door at the end. "Anyone there?" I yell. "Two men are hurt in here. We need help!"

Come to think of it, shouldn't people have come running by now? The cell door didn't exactly explode quietly. The police station has to be full of people, so where are they?

Hurrying back to the police officer, I pull a swipe card and set of keys from his belt. I'm going to need to get through some doors if I'm going to find help.

Rushing to the door at the end of the hallway, I use the swipe card to get it open. Outside is a large, open-plan office with several desks and chairs. There's nobody here, but surely people should still be working? Some of the computers are on and their screen savers haven't kicked in. It's as though all the policemen have disappeared into thin air.

A sickening chill runs through me. Could my magic have done something bad to them? Maybe I killed the two men who were with me, and vaporised everyone else in the police station. The idea makes me want to throw up.

"Please, no." I say aloud, the words little more than a moan. "Let them be okay." I swallow hard, fighting the lump in my throat. I can't afford to fall apart. Not if there's any chance I can still save the men lying on the floor of my cell.

Stumbling toward the door at the far side of the office, I raise my voice and shout at the top of my lungs. "Help! Is anyone here? Is anyone still alive?"

Chapter Twelve

The door at the far end of the office flies open. "Shhh, Saffy. Not so loud."

I gape at the person standing there. The last person I expected to see.

"Aunt Therese?" I say stupidly.

Gone is the zombie apocalypse look—no more black smudges under my aunt's eyes, and no gaunt hollows or sunken cheeks. She looks like she used to before my parents died.

She motions to me. "Come on. We don't have much time." She's wearing cashmere and pearls, and looks so out of place, I have to blink a couple of times to make sure it's really her.

"I can't leave. I think I might have killed a couple of people. They're back here." I turn away from her.

"Saffy!" Her voice rises.

I glance back. "Please, Aunt Therese. They need help." Hoping she'll follow, I head to the fallen medic and policeman. Though fire witches don't have the ability to heal, she's powerful. She'll know what to do.

Thankfully, she follows me into the cell and bends over the two men. Watching her, I spot two blood-red runes, one drawn on each of her arms. White and gold strands of magic weave over her skin, twisting and curling around both her arms. Over one rune, the magic looks strong. The other is weaker, but the tingle I feel in the air seems to be coming from the faint one. Her eyes have a golden glow.

"The men are fine," she says, straightening. "You cast a spell on them?"

I let out a long breath, my legs suddenly weak with relief. "They're not dead? I tried to put them to sleep, but afterwards I couldn't find a pulse on either of them."

"Their hearts are beating, but weakly. They're both in a heavy coma."

My relief disappears. "A coma?" That sounds serious.

"It'll take time for your spell to wear off, but once it does, they'll wake up. There shouldn't be any ill effects."

"You're sure?"

She nods. "We need to go quickly."

I follow her back into the hallway and use the swipe card to let us back into the empty office. "Where is everyone?" I ask.

"No time for questions. We need to keep moving. Magnus is waiting."

Sure enough, when we go through the door at the far end of the office, Magnus is striding toward us. His large frame is crammed into a dark suit that makes him look more like a CEO than the head witch of the Blood Council, though his long gray beard still reminds me of Gandalf. He's frowning at me like it's my fault he's here. I guess it is.

We're in another, larger office, filled with rows of desks and computers. Several chairs have been left in the middle of the rows, as if the people sitting in them got up quickly to leave. One wall has pin boards with photos and case information posted over it, and another wall has a large television playing the local news channel with no sound.

The whole area is eerily empty of people. Instead of being relieved, it creeps me out.

"Where are all the policemen?" I ask.

"Hurry, Sapphira." Magnus sounds grumpy. "Your aunt can only hold them for so long." He motions at the rune on her right arm. Its magic is definitely fading, though the rune on her left arm is still potent, the strands of magic still strong.

"Hold who?" I stride forward to catch up to him.

"The policemen, of course. Therese is channelling a powerful spell."

It takes me a moment to realise what he's talking about. "She's using the Blood Council link to the Veritas?" It's how he got me out of the police station when Sylvia was first murdered.

"Your aunt has convinced them you're innocent and should be set free. They're filling out your release papers." He grasps my arm and pulls me along even faster. I stumble behind him for a few paces before managing to yank my arm free.

"We need to be gone before the spell gets too weak." Aunt Therese hurries beside us. "You'll fade from their memories completely if we can get out of here without them seeing you again. All their files on you and Sylvia have been deleted from their computers. If we leave quickly, your troubles with the law will be over."

"Thank you. That's..." I shake my head, lost for words. "I had no idea you were powerful enough to do something like that."

Magnus huffs out a breath. "Your aunt's a very powerful witch. It's why we never suspected your uncle of wrongdoing."

Aunt Therese gives Magnus a sad look as we go through another set of doors, into the public lobby of the police station. Linoleum floors are paired with plain white walls, and it's just as empty as the rest of the station.

"There was nothing you could have done." Her voice echoes in the silent room. "Jeqabeel had us both in a powerful thrall. Ray was as much a victim as I was."

Magnus snorts his disbelief, and for once I agree with him.

"I doubt it took much convincing for him to give up his morality for the demon," says Magnus. "He was always jealous of his sister. Killing her wasn't such a huge leap for him."

"He was a good man in his own way," says Aunt Therese reprovingly.

The glass front doors of the police station are just ahead, and I still haven't seen a single policeman. "Where did you stash all the people?" I ask curiously.

"In one of the staff rooms. They had a strong desire to have a very important meeting." Aunt Therese lifts her right arm. Only a few thin strands of magic remain. "The Veritas is controlling the spell. I'm just the vessel."

"What about the other rune?" I point to her left arm.

"That's a different spell."

I want to ask what it's for, but Magnus hustles me through the front door, peering around like a villain in a crime movie. He makes hurrying motions with his hands as we jog down the steps toward the street.

Magnus's expensive black BMW is parked at an odd angle in a no parking zone in front of the police station. It's early evening, I'm guessing about seven o'clock, and the street is busy. People are hurrying home, or going out to dinner and drinks. Pedestrians bustle right past, and nobody looks twice at the illegally-parked car.

Now that we're outside, I slow down, needing to know what they plan to do about Xander. "Aunt Therese." I put my hand on her arm to stop her. "Is Xander okay? Do you know where he is? The Unseen did something to make the demon stronger."

She nods. "The Veritas saw it happening in a vision. That's why we came looking for you."

My heart leaps. "Did the Veritas see what the Unseen did with my roommate Jess?"

"Your roommate?" asks Magnus sharply. "What happened to your roommate?"

"I don't know where she is. The Unseen made her vanish, and I need you to help me find her."

Aunt Therese and Magnus exchange a startled look.

"Jess vanished? Has it happened before?" demands Magnus. He stares at me with such ferocity, I blink with surprise.

"Of course Jess hasn't vanished before," I snap, regaining my composure by reminding myself I'm angry with Magnus, despite the rescue. "The Unseen was the one who did the vanishing trick." I frown at him, trying to figure out what his angle might be. "Are you going to help me find her?"

Magnus takes a step toward me, his expression grim. "Tell me exactly what happened. It's important." His hands are fisted at his sides, and he looks less like a bearded CEO and more like an avenging angel.

I narrow my eyes. A moment ago we were in a tearing hurry to get away before the spell wore off. Now he wants to hang around and hear about the Unseen and Jess.

"Why are you acting so worried?" I demand. My stomach turns over as I imagine the worst. "Do you know what he plans to do with her? Has he snatched mundanes before?"

"Just tell me what happened, Sapphira."

"The Unseen was at my place, using magic to help the demon take control of Xander. Jess grabbed him, then they disappeared. That's all I know."

Therese puts a hand on Magnus's arm. "I'm sure she's fine, Magnus."

I glare suspiciously between them, more worried about Jess than ever. "What's going on? What aren't you telling me?"

Magnus ignores my questions. "When did it happen?"

I'm tempted not to answer until he tells me why he's suddenly so concerned about the safety of a mundane he's never met. But something about his expression, the hint of fear behind the menace, makes me reply. "A couple of hours ago. Right before I was arrested."

Magnus turns to Aunt Therese. "We need to find her."

"How?" asks my aunt.

"Perhaps Dallas can—?"

"Okay, time out." Narrowing my eyes at them, I make a 'T' symbol with my hands. "Tell me what's going on. Right now."

"We need to go." Aunt Therese glances around as if realizing we're still on the street. "Magnus, tell her in the car. She deserves to know the truth." She moves to the car's passenger side and opens the door. "As harsh as it sounds, our priority isn't finding Jess. We have to get Xander. If the demon's getting stronger, it's vital we stop it before it destroys us all."

My heart feels like it's breaking. If Jess is still with my crazy dark witch stalker she's in terrible danger, and I'm pretty sure Aunt Therese is talking about turning Xander into stone.

"The time you gave me isn't up yet." Before Aunt Therese can get into the car, I grab her upper arm. "Just give me a little longer to save Xander. I can find a way to get the demon out of him, but I need more time."

Magnus shakes his head. "We must—"

"Hey!" A policeman jogs toward us from a little way down the road. My stomach sinks. It's the officer who arrested me. I'd recognize that nose anywhere.

"What the hell is going on?" Sergeant Nose pulls out his gun as he approaches, frowning at me. "You should be having a blood test, not walking out of the station. Put your hands up. We're going back inside."

Nearby pedestrians run for cover when they see the gun. An old man ducks behind a parked car, while a jogger does an impressive dive into a bush. I wish I had the same options.

I put my hands in the air. I'm the only one who does.

Magnus looks at Aunt Therese with a slight frown, as though the policeman is little more than a minor irritation. "The spell?" he asks.

My aunt shakes her head. "It's too weak. I can't extend it."

"Put your hands up now!" The policeman trains his gun on Magnus, who's clearly not taking his threats seriously. Nose looks jumpy, like he's not sure what's happening. He glances quickly over his shoulder to see if anyone in the station is going to provide backup. I'm tempted to tell him they're all in a staff meeting, but I manage to keep quiet.

Magnus lets out an impatient huff. "We're not under your jurisdiction."

"Magnus, do something." Aunt Therese's whisper is loud enough for the officer to hear. Her expression is tense, like she's exerting a lot of effort. "It's about to wear off. We have to leave."

"It's okay, officer." I force a smile, trying to look as

innocent as I can. "Mayor Trent and the rest of your police buddies realized I didn't do anything wrong, so they let me go. It was all a big misunderstanding."

Nose shakes his head, switching his gun back and forth between Magnus and me. "That's not true. I'm the arresting officer, and they'd never release you without notifying me. Hands *up*."

The last demand is directed firmly at Magnus, who, instead of complying, casually reaches into the pocket of his trousers. My stomach turns over when I catch the flash of a blade. He's pulling out a tiny ceremonial knife, used for drawing blood to cast a spell. He's focused on using magic to get us out of here, but it's the worst thing he could do.

"Put your weapon down or I'll shoot!" The policeman's voice is shrill. His finger tightens on the trigger.

Magnus ignores the policeman and swipes the knife across his palm in a gesture that's so well-practised, it looks a dance move. As his blood wells up, the air around the detective shimmers. Ice crystals form.

The detective shoots.

Instinctively I duck as the shoot rings out, throwing my arms over my head as though I can somehow protect myself from a bullet that way. There's a shocked silence that seems to last a long time. No screams. No shouts. Surely not the normal reaction after a gunshot.

After a moment, when I'm fairly sure I haven't been hit, I look up.

The detective is frozen in place, tiny ice particles laced over his skin. His eyes are wide with surprise and his gun is still trained on Magnus. Or rather, where Magnus was a few moments ago.

My gaze falls to where Magnus is now lying crumpled on the grassy verge. His face is white, and there's a hole in his expensive suit. Blood wells from a wound on Magnus's shoulder. He curses loudly, shattering the silence.

"Magnus." Aunt Therese crouches over him. "You've been shot!"

I look behind us to the station. The gunshot wasn't exactly discreet. My aunt said the spell the Veritas cast is wearing off, which means officers are going to start pouring out of the police station, running to find out who shot a gun right outside.

My survival instincts kick in.

"Come on." I haul Magnus off the ground, trying to be as gentle as possible. "I'm sorry if this hurts, but we have to get out of here." Between us, Therese and I manage to get him into the back of his BMW. I climb into the back seat with Magnus, while Therese jumps in the driver's seat.

I roll up Magnus's jacket and press it hard over the gunshot wound, trying to stem the bleeding. The car's cream leather seat is quickly turning red, and I try not to think about how much blood he's losing.

Therese plants her foot and takes off, just as the first policeman emerges from the station. I'm slammed into the soft leather of the back seat, and Magnus groans.

"Where are we going?" I demand as we pull out into the traffic.

Aunt Therese is frowning at the cars, clearly concentrating on driving, but spares me a quick glance in the rear vision mirror. "We need to get Magnus to a healer."

Magnus curses some more, the sound barely louder than a mutter, his face deathly pale. I've got to hand it to him, he knows a lot of swear words, even if some of them sound like he made them up himself.

Magnus speaks up, his voice strained. "Drop me off,

Therese, then go and get Xander as planned. Nothing's changed. Our first priority is still to deal with Jeqabeel."

"By 'deal with Jeqabeel' you mean you're planning to turn Xander into stone," I snap. "But I won't let you."

Magnus's gaze meets mine, although he still looks pale enough to faint at any minute. "We have to do what must be done."

"You don't have to——"

"Perhaps we could keep Xander under a sedation spell for a while, until we know for sure there isn't an alternative." Aunt Therese sounds conciliatory.

"Don't give the girl false hope." Magnus winces as the car speeds around a corner. "We can't delay any longer, not after the vision the Veritas saw. Encasing the demon in a stone vessel is the best chance we have."

I clench my teeth together, keeping my weight on the gunshot wound though I feel like battering my fists against Magnus's chest instead. "There must be a way to stop the demon without turning Xander to stone."

"There's nothing you can do to save him." Magnus's voice is getting weaker. "You did everything you could. You've been very brave. But it's over." He swallows hard, as if he has to force himself to speak. "There's still a chance for Jess. Tell me exactly what happened when she disappeared." He groans as we go around another corner and I lean too heavily on his wound.

I shake my head, wanting to scream. "First tell me why you're so interested in her."

He lets out a long breath. It's obvious his wound is painful, but I can't be too sympathetic. Not when he's being so unreasonable.

His eyelids flutter closed. When he speaks, it's in a whisper so faint I can barely hear it. "Jess is my daughter."

Chapter Thirteen

I still don't have any answers.

As soon as he delivered his bombshell, Magnus fainted. Now I need him to survive so he can tell me what I have to know.

When we get to the healer's house, I help Aunt Therese carry Magnus in, then pace up and down the witch's living room while she examines him. She has animal magic, and specializes in healing wounds.

My brain feels like it's been run over by a train, and then stomped on by the train driver. Magnus's words keep running through my head, but they make no sense. How can Jess be his daughter? She told me her mother had taken off when she was young, and she didn't get on with her father so she hardly ever saw him. Was that true, or was everything she said just a lie?

"Can Magnus talk?" I snap at the healer, too impatient to wait until she's finished her examination. "I have questions for him."

"Uh-uh." The healer is too distracted by whatever

spells she's casting to do more than grunt, but it sounds like a 'no'.

"Magnus?" I raise my voice, directing it at the figure on the bed. He's in some kind of trance, I guess to keep him from feeling pain. "Does Jess know she's your daughter? Why did she move in with me? Why didn't she tell me you were her father?"

Did you ask her to spy on me? The question is on the tip of my tongue but I can't bring myself to say it out loud.

It would mean that Jess betrayed me, and I can't bear the thought.

"We need to go." Aunt Therese takes my arm. "He'll be here for a while, and we need to get Xander."

And take him back to the council chambers so we can turn him into a statue. She doesn't say the words, but I hear them as clearly as if she had.

I'm not going to let them hurt Xander. Somehow, after we find him, I'll get him away from Aunt Therese and take him somewhere safe from the council. I have no idea how I'll escape from such a powerful witch, but I'll figure that out when I need to.

Just like I'll figure out what's been happening with Jess.

"I want answers," I say, letting Aunt Therese lead me to the door.

"I know you do." She looks sympathetic. "I wish I had some to give you, but Magnus only told me about Jess a couple of days ago. He said after your parents died, he wanted to make sure you were okay. You were so angry with him he didn't think you'd accept help if you knew it was coming from him."

So Jess *was* there to watch me.

To make sure I didn't step out of line.

My breath gets stuck in my chest and for a moment I struggle to breathe. The enormity of her betrayal stirs my rage, and my magic rises with it. It pushes against my control, fighting to get out.

All this time, Jess's been lying to me. I thought she was my best friend. I thought she saved my life. Bile rises up my throat as I think about how often we've hung out together.

Turns out it was all an act.

"Jess knows about magic," I snap. "She's a witch. And she let me believe she wasn't."

I step outside and blink in the sunlight. It feels like my life has been swept out from under me.

"Did you tell her *you* were a witch?" My aunt's tone is careful.

"Of course not. But that's different. I don't want anything to do with witches. Besides, my magic was bound. I may as well have been a mundane."

"Jess doesn't have any magic either."

I frown. "Magnus's daughter doesn't have magic? How can that be?"

Aunt Therese shrugs. "It happens sometimes."

Jess is an outsider, just like me. That makes me feel a little better. At least she wasn't lying about *everything*. But I'll never be able to forgive her, or her father.

Still, my worry for her hasn't gone away. Even if she betrayed me, I need to save her from the Unseen.

When we get back into the car, Aunt Therese slides into the driver's seat, but doesn't leave right away. Instead she hands me something wrapped in tissue.

"What's this?" I ask.

"A gift."

I carefully unwrap the tissue to reveal a narrow piece of bone, about an inch long. There's a hairline crack down one side, as if it were crushed at some point. It looks like it might have come from a small animal.

I shoot my aunt a sideways look. "Um, thanks?" My

voice rises involuntarily, making the word a question. "This is great, but maybe next time you could get me a gift card? Then I could choose my own—"

"It'll protect you from the Unseen."

I hesitate, not wanting to admit that the Unseen has power over me, but it's obvious she already knows. "He has my mother's ring," I tell her.

She nods. "Our bond is weaker outside the council chambers, but you're linked to the rest of the council now. We all felt the tug of the Unseen's control over you and I guessed it was something like that."

I hold up the bone. "This will keep me safe?"

She nods. "As soon as I felt the Unseen's power, I fetched the bone from where I'd hidden it, a place far enough away that the Unseen couldn't scry it out. Retrieving the talisman was the only way to help you." She hesitates, looking down at the bone. "Of course, we were all worried. If he can manipulate you like that, he may be able to strengthen the link and use it to influence the rest of us." She sighs and rubs one tired hand over her face.

"He uses dark magic. You know that, right? How come he's gotten away with it for so long? Surely you must have realized...?"

"We weren't sure until now. And he's become much stronger than we dreamed. The council will deal with him once we've dealt with the demon." There's a pinched look on my aunt's face that I'm struggling to read. "In the meantime, because the bone contains his essence, it has a certain power over him. It's similar to how he's using your mother's ring to control you."

I stare down at the small bone, remembering the way the Unseen caressed the grimoire, and how his intact fingers dipped into his bowl of blood, while his shortened finger barely brushed the surface...

"Wait. This isn't his actual bone, is it?" I swallow a sudden rush of stomach acid. "Tell me it's not his pinky finger."

Aunt Therese starts the car and pulls onto the road. "Keep it close." She doesn't answer the question, but a pink tinge is spreading over her cheeks.

I grimace. Still, carrying a piece of creepy human bone around is a whole lot better than being the Unseen's personal slave. I tuck the tissue back around the bone and push it into the front pocket of my jeans. "How'd you get his finger bone?" I ask.

"You don't want to know."

She's wrong about that. I'm immediately intrigued. "Did you cut it off yourself?"

She doesn't say anything for a while. "He wasn't always like he is now." Aunt Therese sounds wistful. "He used to be a good person."

"You and he….?" My stomach turns. Surely not?

She glances at me and then back at the road. "A long time ago, before your Uncle Ray. Turns out I have terrible taste in men."

I frown, having a hard time imagining my elegant Aunt Therese, wearing her cashmere and pearls, attracted to the Unseen's hideous gray face and sharpened teeth. "He must have been very different," I manage.

"He was intelligent, curious, and excited about the world around him. It was intoxicating to be around. But his interest in the demon dimensions became an obsession, and his thirst for knowledge led him to places he shouldn't have gone."

Her expression makes me blink. Could Aunt Therese and the Unseen really have been a couple? Judging from the softness in her eyes, they definitely have some kind of romantic history. She can't have seen him recently, or she'd be as revolted as I am.

"You know the Unseen's trying to help free Jeqabeel, right?" I try not to sound too judgy.

"Once the council's back at full strength, the Veritas will be able to contain him."

"You're going to turn him into a statue? Do you need a full council for that?" If so, maybe Xander has more time than I thought. If they can't perform the spell without replacing their dead members…

"We can do the spell," Aunt Therese assures me, as though she can read my thoughts. "But without a full council, I doubt we'll be powerful enough to get the Unseen to the council chambers and under our control. Not when he commands dark magic."

I let out a disappointed breath. Xander won't be able to fight the council, even if they're only at a fraction of their full strength. They won't have any trouble turning him to stone.

My only faint consolation is knowing that the council are planning to do the same thing to the Unseen. It's a whole lot better than believing he might always be able to control me unless I carry around part of his finger.

"Thanks for the bone," I say. "It'll be easier to save Jess now. He's probably holding her in his basement, and if both of us go—"

"I'm afraid we don't have time to save Jess now. We're getting Xander."

I shake my head. "We need to help Jess first. The police have Xander, and as sucky as that is, at least they won't hurt him. Jess is the one in the most danger."

"Saffy, if the demon manages to escape Xander's body, it could kill us all."

"Yes, but the Unseen could be doing horrible things to Jess."

"We're not strong enough to fight the Unseen. Our first priority has to be Xander." Her eyes are soft, but her jaw is set and her tone is firm. My heart sinks as I realize she's made up her mind.

"Aunt Therese, please. If you're set on getting Xander first, at least send some witches to the Unseen's house to look for Jess."

"I can't risk it." Her knuckles are white on the wheel. "I'm sorry, Saff. More sorry than you know. But we can't face the Unseen's power. Not yet."

I want to scream. "But you can't just leave her—"

"We have witches ready to join the council, to bring our numbers back up to eight. As soon as we've dealt with Xander, we'll perform the ceremony. Then we'll have the strength to control the Unseen." Aunt Therese lets go of the wheel to squeeze my hand. "Don't worry, Saffy. We'll go after Jess as soon as we can. Magnus is just as worried for her as you are. He's anxious to get her to safety. I promise, we'll do everything in our power."

I nod. Maybe Jess doesn't have any magic, but I could tell Magnus was worried. At least I'm not the only one who wants to rescue her.

When Aunt Therese lets go of my hand to put it back on the wheel, my eyes are drawn to the strands of magic still coiled around the rune on her left arm.

White magic, mixed with gold, like the spell she used to influence everyone in the police station.

Magic channelled from the Veritas.

"What's that for?" I ask, nodding to the rune.

She hesitates. "A spell I hope I won't need." Her tone is reluctant. "But we had to take precautions."

I wait, staring at her.

Ahead is a red light, and she slows down too far in advance, as though she's stopped concentrating on the road. Her gaze flicks to me and she looks almost guilty. Then she lets out a sigh. "If necessary, I can use the spell to contain Xander."

"It's the statue spell?" My voice rises.

She turns to face me. "I'm here to take Xander to the council chambers. He'll be safe there, and my preference is to weave a containment spell that will keep him sedated while we look for a better solution. The statue spell is a last resort. I won't use it. Not if there's any other choice."

I shake my head. "Magnus seemed all too eager to turn Xander to stone."

"Maybe he is, but I'm not." The light turns green and she starts accelerating. "Saffy, of all the awful things the demon did to me, the worst was keeping me from you after your parents died. But I'm here now. I'm on your side." Her brow creases. "Don't you know that you've always been like a daughter to me?"

I stare straight ahead, my heart twisting in my chest. After the explosion, I was heartbroken over the loss of my parents when the council stripped me of my magic. Aunt Therese and I had been close, but at the lowest, most agonizing point in my life, she'd refused to see me. It'd taken everything I had to pick myself up and start again.

Now, to realize she didn't abandon me of her own free will...

Tears rise, hot and insistent behind my eyes, but I blink them away. This is no time to fall apart. Not when Xander needs my help.

Focusing on the road ahead, I realize I don't know where we're headed. "Where's Xander?" My voice sounds a little croaky, and I clear it impatiently, fighting to get control over my emotions. The time for tears was long ago, when I thought my aunt had turned her back on me. Not now, when she could be the only friend I have left.

"His mother pulled some strings to get him admitted to a private hospital, which should make it easier to break him out. There'll be fewer people around." Aunt Therese turns her face away to check there's nobody beside her before changing lanes, and I notice a lot of thin white lines on the back of her neck, running down past the line of her shirt. They're scars. Finely cut lines in her skin, like someone has been slicing into her.

I've never seen them before, and we were close enough when I was growing up that I would have noticed them.

"Did Uncle Ray hurt you?"

Her expression tightens, and I immediately want to take the question back. She lifts a hand to the back of her neck, tugging her shirt up to cover the marks.

"I'm sorry," I say, before she can answer.

When she glances at me, her eyes seem bruised. "The demon had your uncle under its control. Through Ray, it was also able to control me."

"How?" Though I hate making her talk about it, I need to know as much as I can about our enemy.

"Jeqabeel feeds on fear and pain. It managed to produce those feelings in me on a regular basis." The words sound matter-of-fact, but the lines around her mouth deepen. The anguish in her expression makes my chest feel tight. I want to hug her and tell her how sorry I am.

Uncle Ray must have cut her over and over again, feeding the demon's lust for blood while using its power to turn her into a frail, sickly shadow. How many of those scars does she have? Do they cover her whole body?

Jeqabeel must have been feeding on her for *years*.

An image flashes in my mind of the demon ripping

Xander's flesh with his teeth. Xander doesn't have any magic for the demon to feed on. It even said it wanted to kill him, maybe because it thinks that'll help it get inside a new host.

A new, magical host. That's what it needs.

My blood chills, and I swallow a hard lump of fear.

Jeqabeel will kill Xander if it gets the chance. I can only hope whatever guard the police have put on him doesn't slip up, even for a minute.

"Are you all right, Saffy?" Aunt Therese frowns at me, concern in her eyes.

I nod, my mind racing. "The demon has been free before, right?"

She nods. "In the eighteen hundreds. The witches back then banished it into its own thigh bone."

"Why do that, instead of destroying it, or sending it back where it came from?" I can't help sounding bitter. If those witches hadn't just stuck the demon into a bone and called it good, we wouldn't have to deal with Jeqabeel now.

"The demon is immortal. It can't be killed. At least not in this dimension."

"What dimension is it from?"

She shakes her head. "There are a lot of other dimensions. We call all the creatures that inhabit them 'demons', but they're not all the same. This one is particularly powerful. I'm sure the witches who contained it would have sent it back to its own dimension if they could have."

I huff out a loud, frustrated breath. "I've been trying to find a way to send it back where it came from, but if it was too powerful for those witches, what chance do I have? The only solution is to get it out of Xander and trap it in a different vessel." I shake my head. "Problem is, I have no idea how, or if I'd be strong enough."

"You're more powerful than you realize." Aunt Therese

shoots me a sideways glance. "I think you have the potential to be a great witch."

I let out a snort of derision. "You wouldn't say that if you saw the hideous giant statue in my backyard." Not to mention the gargoyle stuck in the library...

"Wielding two types of magic should be impossible, yet you managed it when you fought your uncle and the demon. You surprised us all." She looks like she's proud of me, and my heart does a little flutter. It's been a long time since I had anyone to take an interest in me.

"I don't know how I did that," I admit. "I can't control it."

"With your magic bound, you didn't have any way to learn to control it. But I believe you can master both your animal and earth magic." When she smiles, her eyes crinkle and her whole face looks kind. "You need the right runes to focus all that energy. Now that I'm free of the demon's influence, I'd like to help you. How about we practise together?"

A warm feeling fills my chest. This is the Aunt Therese I remember from before my parents died. We used to be close, and I've missed her more than I can say.

"Thank you, Aunt Therese. I'd like that."

She moves her hand from the steering wheel to cover mine. "There's no changing what's happened, but things can be different from now on. I've watched you grow up, and I've seen your potential. I believe in you, Saffy. If we work together, I think we can find a way to contain the demon without harming Xander."

"Really?" I catch my breath, and for the first time, feel a spark of hope. Aunt Therese is one of the most powerful witches in the state. If she's willing to help, Xander could have a chance after all.

Growing up, I was used to solving every problem with

magic, and when my power was bound, the feeling of being helpless was what I struggled with most.

I remember what it was like to be surrounded with witches who could do anything they wanted. With Aunt Therese on my side, everything will be a whole lot easier.

Aunt Therese pulls the car up outside the front doors of the hospital, in a strict tow-away area that's reserved for ambulances only. She kills the engine, leaves the key in the ignition, and flings her door open. "Xander's in here," she says. "Are you ready to get him back?"

"Ready." I leap out of the car. "Let's go kick some ass."

Chapter Fourteen

A unt Therese and I walk into the hospital like we belong here and know exactly where we're going. The place is busy, with both medical staff and patients bustling around. We breeze past the front desk without being challenged, and I follow my aunt to the elevator, where she punches the button for the third floor.

"How do you know where to go?" I ask as the elevator rises. Aunt Therese has fire magic, and I wouldn't have thought that would give her the ability to track someone down.

"Before we left the council chambers, Dallas helped us locate you both. This is where Xander was then. Hopefully he's still here."

I swallow at the mention of Dallas. I didn't know he could use his air magic to find people. Mind you, there's a lot I don't know about magic.

I'm opening my mouth to tell my aunt about what Dallas did to us in the library, when the elevator doors open and a muffled shout distracts me. It's Xander's voice, but I can't make out what he's yelling.

I exchange a worried glance with my aunt before we hurry up the hallway, rushing past the open doors of several wards where patients are chatting with visitors or watching T.V.

Xander yells again, and we follow the sound around several corners and through a door. Inside a small room, Xander is lying on a bed, his wrists and ankles fastened to the bed's metal rails. His irises are mostly blue, though they're circled with red, as though the demon is fighting for control.

"Get away," he's shouting. "Don't touch me! It wants to hurt you. It'll kill you!"

His mother is bending over him, her eyes wide and her face pale. "Please stop, Xander," she pleads. "This isn't you. Wherever you've gone, please come back."

Therese moves forward, and the mayor looks up, her face hardening when she sees me behind my aunt. "What the hell are you doing here?"

"We've come to save Xander." Aunt Therese sounds calm.

"She's the one who did this to him." Xander's mother points an accusing finger at me.

"She's just as much a victim as Xander." Aunt Therese puts her hands out in a placating gesture.

Xander's face contorts and his eyes roll into the back of his head. When they roll back, his irises are blood red.

"Sapphira and Theresa." His slow drawl sounds smug and he gives us a horrible smirk. "You have no idea what's coming, do you? I'm so pleased you're here. I'm going to enjoy watching you die."

My hands clench into fists. "Stop it," I growl.

Xander closes his eyes. A moment later, he flicks them open. His irises are pale blue once more, and anguish is carved into every line of his face.

"You all have to leave right now." Xander's voice is his own again. "He's coming. He's so close, he'll be here any minute. You have to go."

"Who's coming?" asks Aunt Therese.

"I'm not leaving without you." I say at the same time.

"It's too late for me. Just go." Xander's irises glitter under the bright hospital lights and I can see the demon just under the surface, trying to take control again.

I rush to the bed, wanting to be near him, wishing there were some way I could help him fight the monster inside. "It's not too late."

But Xander's mother steps in front of me, pushing me away. "You've done enough damage. Stay away from him." She raises her voice, shouting toward the closed door. "Somebody help! I need help! These people shouldn't be in here." Then she moves toward her handbag, which is on the chair by Xander's bed. "I'm calling the police."

Aunt Therese grabs Mayor Trent's arm, and I feel the tingle of magic. "Is it getting hot in here?" she asks.

Xander's mother tugs at her grip, but her face reddens and beads of perspiration appear on her brow. "It's hot," she splutters. "It's too hot in here."

I can't feel any change of temperature, but my aunt nods, her expression sympathetic. "It's a lot cooler outside. You'll feel better if you find a bathroom and splash some cold water on your face."

She lets the mayor go, and I spot a smear of blood on the woman's arm where my aunt held her. Xander's mother takes off through the door without another word, leaving us alone with her son.

"Is she going to be okay?" Xander's voice is raspy.

"Of course. She'll be back to normal in a minute or two. We need to get out of here quickly, before she returns with reinforcements." Aunt Therese moves behind his hospital bed. "At least this thing has wheels." She unlocks the brakes and grabs hold of the bed's back rail. "We can just wheel you out—"

A loud explosion makes us both stagger. It's lucky we're both holding the bed, or we might have ended up on the floor. The building shudders, as though an earthquake has hit, then a siren wails. Aunt Therese and I stare at each other, wide-eyed.

"What was that?" she shouts over the noise of the siren.

Before I can answer, a second, louder explosion rocks the building, making me stumble again. Over the siren, I hear screams, then someone shouting. I cross to the window, which looks out over the hospital's entrance. People are streaming out of the building.

Behind us, Xander gives a nasty laugh. His irises have gone red again. "He's here," he drawls. "And when he kills you, I'll take your blood and your power."

"Who's here?" I ask. Then I answer my own question. "The Unseen."

Xander laughs again, his face twisted into a dreadful mask. I can't bear to see the demon's glowing eyes and what it's doing to him. I have to look away.

Aunt Therese's face has paled. "If the Unseen takes Xander, he'll unleash Jeqabeel. I won't let that happen." She draws a ceremonial knife from her pocket and slices her left arm, just above the rune that's still potent with magic. "I'm sorry, Saffy. I thought we had time to look for another way. But we can't let the Unseen have access to the demon." As her blood runs down to the rune, the strands of magic glow brighter, writhing over her flesh.

I step in front of her, ready to grab her arm, to wipe away the rune. "I won't let you do it. We can save him. Let's stop wasting time and get him out of here."

"Saffy, I understand, I really do. But there's a lot at stake, and we can't afford to make a mistake. I'm sorry." Aunt Therese's eyes are soft, her expression full of sympathy. I really believe she knows how I feel. She knows how hard this is, and believes we have to do it anyway.

I swallow, trying not to doubt myself. I can't give up on Xander, no matter what she thinks.

"What if turning him to stone turns out to be the mistake?" I ask. "Who's to say the demon can't feed on your magic while you're casting the spell? Instead of stopping Jeqabeel, you could be giving it power." I talk in a rush, all too aware of how strong my aunt is, and how easily she got rid of Xander's mother. "We don't know enough about the demon to be sure it's the right thing to do."

She shakes her head, but I catch a flicker of uncertainty in her eyes. "Magnus was certain—"

"Magnus could be wrong." Her magic is still in check, still seething around her arm, so I keep talking. "We need more time to be certain we're doing the right thing—"

Another explosion rips through the building, much louder this time. We both duck as bits of the ceiling fall, and I grab Aunt Therese, trying to shelter her from the worst of it.

"Let's get out of here," I yell. Without waiting for her to agree, I shove Xander's bed through the door and into the corridor. It's almost deserted outside. Most people probably fled when the alarm went off.

I turn the unwieldy bed to head down the corridor the same the way we came in, hoping the explosions came from the other direction. Xander is fighting against the straps binding him to the bed, shaking it and making it harder to push. I shove it along as fast as I can, struggling to keep the bed moving smoothly.

The bright overhead lights flicker on and off. It's dark outside, so when they go out, it's hard to see. Hopefully they won't go out altogether.

We round a corner, into the junction of four connecting corridors. There are a few doctors and nurses running down one corridor, helping patients who are in wheelchairs and on crutches. The hallway to our left is the one we took to get to Xander, but parts of the ceiling have fallen down and are littering the floor. To steer the bed that way will be difficult.

"This way," I say, choosing the corridor that others have taken. They must know how to get out.

I try not to think about the people who have already been hurt by the Unseen's destruction of the hospital. It'll only get worse if we let him get to Xander and the demon.

We're almost at the end of the corridor when the stair-well doors burst open in front of us as if there's been an explosion on the other side. Aunt Therese and I are knocked backward from the blast. We slam against the wall. Xander yells, but it's not a sound of fear. He sounds exalted.

The Unseen strides out of the doorway, his skinny frame wrapped in a long coat. When I first saw him, he looked like a kindly old grandfather, but he's not bothering to disguise his true ugliness anymore. His gray skin is covered in scars and scabs and his lips are pulled back from his disgusting teeth in a triumphant snarl.

"You're finally here." Xander yanks his arms up as far as his restraints will allow. "Free me now!"

The Unseen inclines his head in a half-bow. "Of course, my lord."

"You'll need to get through us first," I scramble to my feet. "I'm not giving you Xander."

The Unseen gives me an amused look. "Sapphira. So nice to see you again."

I pull Aunt Therese to her feet and his amusement slips. "Therese. You're here." The Unseen's steps falter. There's a new quality to his voice that I can't decipher. How long has it been since they've seen each other? The piece of finger bone in my pocket feels heavy with a history that I don't know.

"I wish I could say it was nice to see you." Aunt Therese's voice sounds hollow, and I can tell she's shocked. "You're a shell of the man I once knew."

The Unseen's expression hardens. "I'm one hundred times greater than the pathetic witch I was all those years ago. That stunt you pulled would never work on me now." He sniffs the air, like he's Hannibal Lector looking for his next meal. "It seems you still have your little memento of me. How sweet." His eyes glitter with a dark menace that has nothing to do with his magic, and a shiver runs along my skin.

"I thought it would be enough to protect you from yourself," says Aunt Therese. "I can see I was wrong." She's touching the rune on her left arm, but the strands of magic are no longer coiled around it. Blood is smeared across her skin, and the rune is a mess. The force of the blast must have destroyed it.

The Unseen growls. "I spent many long years trying to get around your spell. To break the magic binding me to that damn bone."

"I didn't mean for it to focus you toward the darkness. I thought it might ease your mind, allow you some peace." Aunt Therese's face is pale, and she's visibly shaking. I reach out to take her hand, trying to give her comfort. Her palm is sticky with blood, and I flinch back, changing my mind about holding her hand. But she grabs me before I can pull away, hanging on so tightly to my fingers that I wince. I didn't notice her cutting herself again, but her other hand is also bright red. She must have made deep cuts in both palms when I wasn't looking.

"*Peace?*" he sputters. "You bound me so I could have no peace. I was throttled by your arrogance and pride. You didn't like my path, so you chose one for me. Who are you to do that?" The Unseen spits on the floor beside him. "No one. You're nothing to me. I heard what happened to you at Ray's hands, and I was glad. *Glad.*"

"You always had a problem with jealousy." Aunt Therese doesn't take her eyes off the Unseen. It feels like they're trying to glare each other to death.

"What? Jealous of Ray? A man too weak to take power and then skinned alive by his own niece? I think not."

"Where's Jess?" I cut in. "What have you done to her?" I'm cursing myself for not giving the police the Unseen's address. If he left Jess alone at his house to come here, they might have been able to save her.

In front of us, Xander makes an impatient noise. "Enough," he snaps, his voice echoing down the corridor. "Release me!"

When the Unseen's eyes dart to him, Aunt Therese tugs on my hand. "I need to pull some of your magic through the council bond," she whispers from the side of her mouth.

I squeeze her hand in reply. She can have anything she likes, as long as she beats the Unseen.

Then I get the unpleasant sensation of having someone else inside my head. Except she's not in my head, she's inside the council magic that's been lying dormant inside me. She unwinds it out of me like it's a ball of string. A powerful, sizzling, about-to-go-nuclear, ball of string. Until now I hadn't realized how much energy was in the council bond.

As she pulls it out of me, it feels invasive and wrong, and part of me wants to try to stop her. But I manage to hold myself together.

Aunt Therese holds up one hand, fire forming in her palm. Waves of heat radiate out from the fire, and I break out in a sweat. I lean away from her magic, trying not to get burned by the sheer force of her power. She keeps holding tight to my hand. Maybe she needs the physical contact, but I feel like I'm being cooked alive.

The fireball grows until it's enormous, while the Unseen draws runes in the air in front of him, his bloody finger leaving a glistening red trail of magic after it, as though he's drawing on the surface of a window.

The fireball in my aunt's palm is so big, I have to turn my face away to keep its heat from searing my face. I want to call out, to tell her to stop, but my lungs feel like they're about to burst into flames.

My aunt launches the fireball at the Unseen.

The fire hits the runes he's drawn in front of him, and they push the flames to either side of where he's standing. The fire leaves scorch-marks along the corridor's walls.

Fire is already forming in Therese's hand again, the heat building. She drags more of the council's magic out of me.

The fire is so hot and bright, I can barely see the Unseen. He's drawing more runes, and red magic flares toward us as he launches his own magic attack. The red tendrils don't go far, though. They're burned up before they can get close to us. They can't get through the intense force of Aunt Therese's fire magic.

She thrusts her hand further in front of her, focused on the flames that are reflected in her irises. I want to watch, but it feels like my eyes are on fire. I have to squeeze them shut. The council magic is almost depleted; she's taken as much as she can.

I hope it's enough.

The air sizzles around us, the air so hot I can barely breathe. Sweat is dripping down my back, and my palms are so slippery I have to concentrate on keeping hold of Aunt Therese's hand.

My aunt jerks as she launches another fireball, and the heat immediately eases. I open my eyes and gape at the devastation. The walls and floor in front of us are burning. The corridor is an inferno.

The Unseen is nowhere to be seen. Surely there's no way he can still be alive.

"Come on," I yell hoarsely, the words rasping up my throat like sandpaper. "Let's get out of here."

I yank the bed, pulling Xander back the way we came. When we're far enough from the flames, I rush to the other end of the bed so I can shove it in front of me. Then we run as fast as we can, hurtling down the long corridor while Xander makes it harder by tugging on the restraints that are holding him down.

We round the corner, and collide with two nurses rushing out of one of the wards.

"Come on," says one, a dark-haired older lady. "This way." She takes hold of the bed and helps me push it forward. But the corridor branches just ahead, and I can see the elevators down one end, the opposite way to where she's trying to steer us.

"That way," I tell her, nodding toward the elevators.

She shakes her head. "The elevators are off-limits in an emergency. The stairwell is there. See?" She points down the other hall, to a door at the far end.

"That's not going to work," says my aunt. "We can't untie Xander, and we can't get the bed down a stairwell."

"We need to untie him to get him out of the building. I'll help." The other nurse fumbles with the restraints around Xander's wrist, but strands of golden magic snake out from Aunt Therese's still-bloody palm, and the nurse pulls back, clutching her hand as though it's burned.

"Take the stairs," I tell them. "Save yourselves, don't worry about us."

The nurses both hesitate.

"Go!" orders Aunt Therese, her voice booming through the corridor.

Both nurses look at each other, then hurry toward the stairwell.

We go in the other direction, and as soon as we reach the elevators, I slam my hand down on the button. I keep hitting it, trying to speed up the time it takes for the car to get to the third floor. A sign on the wall warns not to use the elevators if the alarm sounds. The siren's still going off, the noise deafening in the narrow corridor, but we have no choice.

The elevator dings for our floor just as the two nurses reach the stairwell door at the far end of the other corridor, near the corner. Before they can get the door open, there's a loud roar, and they're both thrown backward as though by a blast of air. They hit the wall behind them, and collapse to the ground.

The Unseen stalks around the corner. Smoke swirls after him, like the corridor is alight behind him. He's covered in ash and smoke, but otherwise looks none the worse for having been set on fire. When he sees us, his mouth stretches into an unholy grin that shows off his mouthful of sharpened teeth.

Behind us, the elevator doors slide open with a ding.

The Unseen strides toward us, his gait surprisingly quick for such a wizened old man. Behind him, the two nurses are struggling to their feet.

"Get in the elevator," orders Therese, her knife in her hand.

The elevator doors start to shut, so I jam the bed into them. The doors hit the bed and open again, and I shove it further inside. The bed only gets halfway before it stops, its wheels stuck.

The two nurses make another dash for the stairwell door. The Unseen turns, lifting his hand. Red tendrils snake from his bloody palm, and one of the nurses, the older dark-haired woman, takes awkward steps toward him, as if she's being dragged against her will. Her face is contorted with fear, and her arms are twisted as if they're the only body part that still understands which way she wants to go.

The second nurse reaches the stairwell door, tears it open and disappears. As it slams behind her, the older nurse reaches the Unseen.

He doesn't look strong enough to hold her but he loops his arm around her neck and presses a knife to her throat. All the blood has drained from the nurse's face. She grabs his arm, but otherwise she doesn't struggle. I don't think she can move.

"Let the woman go," demands Aunt Therese.

"Cut her throat," drawls Xander.

The Unseen's knife pierces the nurse's skin, and a trickle of blood runs down her neck, soaking the edge of her white uniform. Seething red tendrils of magic cover her body like creeping vines. The nurse opens her mouth in a silent scream, but no sound comes out. Her body and voice are locked tight by the spell.

The vibration of the Unseen's dark magic lifts all the hairs on my arms.

"Bring Xander to me, Sapphira." The Unseen's voice is filled with power. The red tendrils snake toward me, and his compulsion tugs at me.

I thrust my hand in my pocket to grab hold of his finger bone. "You have no power over me," I spit, hoping it's true. "You can't make me do anything."

He snarls when he realizes I'm not obeying his command. Then his knife digs deeper into the nurse's neck and more blood gushes. Panic rises in my chest as I realize he means to kill her. I start toward them, intending to tear the nurse away from him, but before I can take more than a step Aunt Therese thrusts out her own blood-streaked hand. A fireball sizzles over her palm, although this one is smaller than before. "Let the woman go," she demands in a strong, carrying voice.

Then, pitched low so only I can hear, she murmurs, "Get Xander into the elevator, Saffy. *Now.*"

I hesitate, still poised to rush the Unseen, wanting to wrestle the nurse away from him. But then, without warning, the Unseen stabs the knife deep into the nurse's neck. Her eyes go wide, shocked and terrified. Then her head sags. The Unseen pulls the knife out and lets her go. She drops to the floor while I stare at her body in horror. My chest squeezes like iron bars are tightening around it.

"Get in the elevator," hisses my aunt.

The urgency in her voice gets me moving. The elevator's doors are opening and closing on the sides of Xander's bed. I shove as hard as I can and the bed shoots into the elevator.

"I'm in," I tell Aunt Therese. "Come on."

The Unseen holds up both hands. They're thickly coated in the nurse's blood, and his red tendrils of magic have become so dark they're almost black. Fire erupts from his entire body, as though he's been set alight. "You're no match for me," he shouts at Aunt Therese. "I'll send back your flames a hundred times stronger."

I grab the elevator doors before they can close. "Come on, Aunt Therese. Get in. Hurry."

She glances back at me. "Go, quickly. You can't let the Unseen take Xander."

"But you have to come—"

Aunt Therese hurls her fireball at the Unseen and it slams into him with a loud whoomph. For a moment the Unseen disappears in flame, and I dare to hope he's hurt. Then he stalks out of the fire, not even singed. He lifts one hand, flashing his horrible, gleeful grin.

"I'll send back your flames," he crows again. The fireball that forms on his outstretched palm is far bigger than the one my aunt threw at him. Its core looks black instead of red, as though he's set a cannonball alight and is about to launch it at her.

"Aunt Therese, get out of the way!" I yell.

She steps in front of the still-open elevator doors but doesn't make any move to get inside. "Go now," she orders me. "Don't wait."

The Unseen throws the fireball at Aunt Therese.

She lifts her arms wide, her head falling back. The fireball hits her and she takes the flames into herself, swallowing them whole. I hold my breath, praying she has the power to absorb all that fire.

For a moment the flames are so bright, I have to shield my eyes. An intense wave of heat burns my skin. I keep my eyes on Aunt Therese, desperately hoping she's okay. Surely she can handle the flames? She's a powerful fire witch, after all.

She's standing with her back to me, her arms

outstretched. Thin black marks appear all over her skin, like fine cracks. As though she's breaking into pieces. Fear contracts my chest, making it hard to breathe.

"Aunt Therese?" I whisper, my throat tight.

For a moment, nothing happens. Then Aunt Therese's body disintegrates in front of me. Where she was standing, black ash swirls.

I stagger backward, my hands flying to my mouth as I make a keening sound I can't control.

The elevator doors slide shut.

As I scream, all I can hear is the sound of Xander's laughter.

Chapter Fifteen

Once out of the elevator, I manage to push Xander's bed toward the car, though my limbs feel completely numb, like my body belongs to someone else.

All I can see is a swirl of black ash. Aunt Therese turned to dust. My aunt was a good person. She didn't deserve to die like that.

It doesn't seem real. Aunt Therese can't be gone.

I feel sick. Just when she escaped from the tyranny of Uncle Ray and Jeqabeel, just when she had her life back, she's killed. I don't know how she could be so brave. She stepped in front of that fireball to save me and Xander.

Jeqabeel tortured her for years, feeding on her power and draining her magic, and she still had compassion for Xander, even with the demon inside him. She was the only one willing to help me.

And now she's gone.

"Saffy?" Xander's eyes are blue again and his expression is full of pain. "Are you okay?"

I shake my head, stopping beside the car. Behind me,

the hospital is alight, black smoke filling the air, and flames shooting out the top windows. The flames are bright against the dark night sky. At any moment, the Unseen will come out after us. The one thing I know is that I can't let him get Xander. If I do, my aunt will have died for nothing.

"I need to get you in the car," I tell him.

"Keep me tied up," he warns. "I don't know how long I can hold back the demon."

I unbuckle his leather wrist restraints from the bed and use one of them to secure his hands in front of him. As soon as I undo the buckles on his ankles, Xander jumps off the bed. "Put me in the trunk."

"But—"

"Hurry, Saff." His eyes are already starting to glow again and I pull open the trunk and help him in. When I touch him, the demon's voice is louder than ever, like a knife cutting into my brain, and the burning that sears up my arms is so painful, it's all I can do not to scream.

Once Xander is lying down, I pull another strap tight around his ankles. With a third, I fasten his ankle and wrist restraints to each other, pulling his knees up so all four limbs are bound together. Even as I slam the trunk closed, his eyes are red and his face contorted, the demon back in control.

I race to the driver's side and dive in, squealing the tires as I pull away. In my rear vision mirror, I spot the Unseen striding out of the hospital's front doors, but by that time I'm already in traffic, just one more car lost in a steady stream.

Thumps and loud shouts come from the trunk. Obscenities and threats, muffled but still sufficiently gruesome to make me shudder. I'm shaking so hard that when I loosen my grip on the steering wheel, my hands drum against it. The cars ahead of me blur as I blink tears away.

I don't know where to go.

Aunt Therese said that Dallas found Xander at the hospital, which means the council can track me. Maybe the Unseen can find me too. So where can I go that's safe from all of them? Somewhere warded, where their magic can't penetrate?

There's only one place I can think of.

I turn right at the next street, then plant my foot and weave through the traffic until I finally pull up outside Sylvia's house. The sun's going down and it's starting to get dark. The windows are black and empty, and a forlorn piece of crime scene tape hangs limply from Sylvia's front door, only fastened on one side. I doubt anybody's been here since I rescued Ratticus. As her only living relative, the house belongs to me now. I just hope Sylvia's wards are still active.

When I open the trunk, Xander glowers out at me with his eyes glowing red. My heart sinks. With the demon in control, how will I get Xander inside?

Before I can come up with a plan, Xander lunges at me. With his wrists and ankles bound together, he manages to use one elbow to haul himself awkwardly out of the trunk. He falls hard, thumping onto the ground. Jeqabeel doesn't care how much he hurts Xander's body. All he cares about is trying to hurt me.

I bend to grab his arms and restrain him on the ground, clenching my teeth against the agony of his touch and the demon's voice that slices into my mind.

"You have one chance to live. Defy me and I'll destroy you. Your agony will be endless. Your screams will..."

Black, oily magic curls up my arms. The pain makes

me gasp, and the magic turns my stomach, so it's all I can do not to pull away.

Xander struggles, trying to flip us over so he can get on top of me. My stonemason work has made me strong, far stronger than most, but Xander is tall and powerfully built. If he wasn't bound so tightly, there's no way I'd be able to overpower him.

"Submit or die," he hisses aloud, the voice in my ears matching the one cutting into my head. Xander's teeth snap together as he cranes his neck forward, trying to bite me.

My skin feels like it's on fire, the pain unbearable. Worse, the magic is covering my body, sinking into my flesh. I grit my teeth and hang on anyway, trying to lift him. But he's too heavy to carry, and if I try to drag him over the sidewalk and up Sylvia's path, I'll scrape off several layers of his skin.

With a scream, I let go of him, jumping back and brushing my body as though I can get rid of the demon's disgusting magic that way.

"Xander," I say desperately. "Please, Xander. Are you in there?"

Red eyes glare back at me. "Your boyfriend's gone," spits the demon. "Release me and beg for your pathetic life."

I drag in a breath. There's only one thing I can think of to do, and it's likely to get me killed. But what choice do I have?

"Okay, I'll let you go. Don't move and I'll unbuckle your restraints." I reach down to where his wrists and ankles are fastened together.

The demon watches me, triumph and murder in its eyes. I can feel its hatred for me rising off Xander in waves. But it holds itself back, waiting to be released.

There are three straps. One binding his ankles, one his wrists, and one holding his wrists and ankles together.

Slowly I unfasten the strap that will let his wrists and ankles separate. He stretches full length, offering his wrists next, waiting for me to unbuckle them. Instead, I undo the one around his ankles before leaping back.

"That's enough." I take a step backward up Sylvia's path. "Now, go. Leave me alone."

Xander scrambles to feet with his wrists still bound, his face twisted in a sneer. "You're mine now, witch."

He lunges for me, faster than I expected, and I jump back before spinning around. I bolt toward Sylvia's house. He runs after me, shoes thudding behind me as I rush up her front path and charge through her wards. I scramble up her steps to her front door and swing around toward Xander, my chest heaving. This is it. If my gamble hasn't worked, I'm dead.

Xander is standing at the top of the steps, close enough to touch me. He's blinking, his eyes pure blue and his expression lined with pain.

"Saffy?" he whispers.

I sag, my legs suddenly so weak I almost slide down the door onto the floor. Sylvia's wards were created to keep out anyone magical that meant her harm. As her heir, the wards now protect me, but I had no idea if they'd work on the demon that's inside Xander.

I'd give just about anything to hug Xander and sob with relief to have him back instead of the demon. But I still don't dare to touch him. Instead, I turn to the door and pull out Sylvia's spare key from its hiding place above the lintel. "Come on," I say. "Let's go inside."

He makes an agonized sound. "I can feel the demon inside me, trying to get out. It's much stronger now. I don't know how long I can keep it back."

"I know." I push open the door and walk down the hallway. "But I think… I hope… being inside might help."

In Sylvia's living room, I tug out the right book from the bottom shelf of her enormous bookcase, and the portal to her athenaeum opens. It's a doorway to a place outside our world. The only place we may have a chance of being safe. "Come on," I say again, and step through into darkness.

The small, magical room lights up. Inside it, Sylvia's grimoires line the walls. Xander steps through behind me and I turn to him. "The athenaeum exists outside of normal space, and because these grimoires are so dangerous, it's heavily warded."

Xander's eyes widen. "It's gone. The voice in my head. I can't hear the demon anymore."

"You can't?"

"Oh God, Saffy. You have no idea…" He breaks off, shaking his head. "It wanted to hurt you. Not just you, but everyone."

"I know. I'm so sorry." It's a risk, but I need to know for sure whether the room's wards are keeping the demon fully suppressed, so I reach out and touch Xander's arm, waiting for pain to spread up my arm and Jeqabeel's voice to whisper in my mind.

Nothing.

There's no whisper. No sound or sensation at all.

The breath leaves my body, and I throw my arms around him, hugging his whole body awkwardly over his bound arms. "You have no idea how much I've needed to touch you."

His brings his bound wrists up awkwardly. "Saffy, be careful. The demon's still inside me. We can't be sure it won't find a way to take over again."

"I'm going to release your hands."

He jerks them away. "No, don't. We can't risk it."

I slip under his arms and press my face against his chest, just to feel his beating heart. He feels warm, and comfortable, and *right*. "I'm going to fix this. I'll find a way to get the demon out of you for good." I'm not sure who I'm trying to convince, myself or Xander.

I can only hope Sylvia's wards also stop magical tracking spells, so we'll have some time here before anyone finds us.

"Whatever this room is doing to control the demon, at least it's working for the moment." Xander lets out a ragged breath. "Now all you have to do is kill me."

Chapter Sixteen

I draw back, stunned.

Xander looks haggard, defeated, and deadly serious.

"What?" I manage. "No."

"Saffy, you have to. It's the only way." Xander swallows hard, then drags in a loud, uneven breath. "The demon is... terrifying. The things it wants to do, the way it thinks."

"I'm not giving up. I'm going to find a way to defeat it."

Xander's eyes are filled with so much pain and sadness, it breaks my heart. "If you kill me in here, even if the demon survives, the room might trap it, and—"

"The answer's no." I glare at him. "Don't you dare quit on me." I feel sick. It seems like everywhere I turn, there's someone telling me to give up, to let Xander die. I didn't expect it from Xander himself.

"It's not about quitting, Saff." He reaches out with his bound hands and grasps one of mine. "It's about saving the people we care about. If the demon gets free, it'll destroy the world."

"We can still find a spell to lock the demon away somehow, I know we can." I gesture at the grimoires surrounding us. "There must be something that can help us in Sylvia's books. She kept the most powerful ones locked in here, so if there's anything that can help, it's on these shelves."

It feels like a thin straw to grasp, and part of me can't help but wonder if Xander's right. Even the Blood Council members working together were no match for the demon. What makes me think I can do better?

"It's over. We tried. Now it's time to be sensible and do what we have to." Xander's voice is resigned, and it breaks my heart. I'm the one who got him into this. If he'd never met me, he'd still be the hotshot new detective on the Baltimore force, fighting the bad guys, oblivious to the magical undercurrent in the city.

He certainly wouldn't be talking about killing himself to save us all.

"I'm not giving up," I insist. There's no way I'm going to let it end here. As long as I have breath in my body, I'm going to fight for Xander.

I reach over and pull out the grimoire closest to me, thumping it down on the table. When I open it, a puff of smoke escapes, making me cough. The pages are singed, and so crumbly they all but fall apart in my hands.

It's a very old grimoire, obviously written by a fire witch. The spells are mostly about how to make fire burn bigger, brighter, and hotter, even from long distances, and I can't help thinking of Aunt Therese. If only she could have protected herself from the Unseen's dark magic.

"Nothing in here," I mutter, slamming it shut. "But there are plenty more books on the shelf."

Xander looks at me sadly, his eyes melting into mine. I glare back at him and grab another grimoire.

This one is so light, it floats off the bookshelf onto the table and flutters open of its own accord. Air magic. The runes inside it drift breezily across its pages as though a gust of wind will blow them away. There's nothing useful in the book, but I notice a few different kinds of location spells, one of which can be used to detect the air somebody's drawing into their lungs.

Interesting, but not what we need.

I don't look up at Xander. I know he's waiting for me to agree to do what he wants, but I never will. Not even if killing him is the only way to save the world.

"Saffy—"

I shake my head. "Don't say it."

Then I feel his hand on my arm. "Leave those books for a minute. Please. I don't think I have much time left."

I heave a sigh. He's right. Our stay in Sylvia's athenaeum will be short, because the council and the Unseen are both coming for us. I have no doubt they'll eventually find us here. If nothing else, the spell Magnus placed on us will draw us back to the council after the original forty-eight hours have elapsed. How many hours have already slipped by? I've lost track.

Reaching for Xander's arms, I start unbuckling the straps around his wrists.

"Don't." He jerks away. "It's not safe."

"We both need to rest while we can. You won't be able to if you're tied up." I glare at him, daring him to defy me. "Besides, I've had enough of not being able to touch you. It sucks, and I'm over it."

"But if the demon takes control again…"

"I'll take that chance."

I grab the strap again and get it undone. As soon as it falls off, I move against him. The feel of his arms tightening around me makes me sigh aloud. I've been longing to be this close to him. To be able to touch him.

I slide my hands underneath his T-shirt, needing to feel the warmth of his skin against mine. His lips come down hard on mine, as though he's falling into me from a great height.

"It's okay," he whispers against my lips. "Just know that I'm not afraid to die. Not any more."

"Stop. Please, let's pretend there's nothing wrong. For a little while, at least."

I close my eyes tightly, forcing away images of the demon, of the Unseen, of my Aunt Therese, and of Jess. I stumble over the thought of Jess, my mind snagging on my worry. But as much as I want to find Jess and make sure she's okay, I can't leave Xander here alone. I'll have to trust Magnus will take care of her. There's nothing else I can do.

Right now, I'm drained, exhausted, and heart sick. I need to forget everything else so I can catch my breath. All I want is to lay down my overwhelming worries for a few minutes, and pretend everything's okay.

All that exists is this moment, just the two of us. Xander and me together, the way we should be.

The way we might never be again.

He kisses me hungrily, his lips hot and demanding. One of his hands goes into my hair, the other moves down my back. He's so tall and wide, I feel like I'm enclosed inside my own Xander-cave. It makes me feel safe. And needy. I want more of him. I want him to make me forget every-thing except how good he feels.

"Saffy," he groans.

The sound of his voice stokes the fire in my belly. I slide my hands further around his waist, pulling him even closer.

"Nothing else exists," I say out loud. "This room is the whole world. Let's pretend we're the first people to ever live."

"Adam and Eve?"

"Exactly."

He raises his eyebrows. "Can I make a joke about encountering a giant snake?"

It shouldn't be possible for me to smile, but somehow I do. If Xander can joke with me, maybe there's hope for us yet.

He moves his mouth down, kissing my neck and throat, and my entire body sighs into his. Everything's gone so terribly wrong and we're on the brink of disaster. It shouldn't be possible for us to let it all go. And it definitely shouldn't be possible for us to find a little happiness in the midst of so much crazy. But we're in the eye of the cyclone, holding on to each other.

I need this. I need *him*.

"Saffy." He pushes his hand into my hair, and pulls his face back to look at me. "When we're together, it seems like everything could be okay."

"It will be."

"If only we could stay here forever." He gives me the saddest smile I've ever seen. "But you have to promise to kill—"

I press my lips against his, kissing away the rest of his request. "No talking," I murmur against his lips. "In our version of Eden, Adam can't talk. He can only grunt. And use his hands."

Xander obliges me by making a grunting sound and lifting my top to stroke my torso.

"That's better." I demonstrate exactly how much better it is by sighing as I kiss him. "That feels good."

Xander makes a sound deep in the back of his throat. "If Adam could talk, he'd tell you how beautiful you are."

"He can talk a little. Eve taught him a few words. Beautiful happens to be one of them."

He cups my face in his hands. "So beautiful."

My heart swells. I thought I was getting to know Xander pretty well, but he keeps surprising me. If he can be sweet and playful when we're staring down the barrel of a demon apocalypse, how great would it be doing this with him on a regular Saturday night?

Dammit, if it's the last thing I do, I want to find out.

I lift his shirt higher so I can run my fingers over his ridged abs. "You're beautiful too," I tell him.

I love the way he smiles, the way his lips tug up and one cheek dimples.

"You sure that's the right word, Eve?" He cocks one eyebrow. "I think Adam's too manly to be beautiful."

"Adam's very pretty." I can't resist teasing him a little as I run my hand over the hard slab of his chest. "Cute?" I pinch his nipple, making him drag in his breath. "Delightful?"

He kisses me so intently, so deeply and passionately, that when the kiss finally ends, I'm breathless and weak with need. Then he lowers me down to the floor and folds his body over me, careful not to crush me.

"You're perfect," I murmur into his mouth.

This time, I've chosen the right word. The word describes how well we fit together, and if I let myself think about it, that fact alone will make me cry. But I won't let myself think about anything but how right this feels. How wonderful Xander feels against me, with his lips on mine. And how I never want this night to end.

Chapter Seventeen

I wake up slowly, groggy and disorientated. A sharp pain shoots down my shoulder as soon as I move.

Opening my eyes, I discover that I'm nestled against Xander on the floor of Sylvia's athenaeum. I try moving away gently, but his eyes flick open.

"Hey," he murmurs sleepily.

"Hey." If things were different, I'd stay right where I was. But I didn't mean to fall asleep in the first place, and it feels like we've slept for hours.

I sit up and stretch. "I don't know what time it is, but I'm so stiff, we must have slept far too long."

"That's okay." He sits up too, stretching his head from side to side as though his neck hurts. "If those were my last hours, that was exactly how I wanted to spend them."

"Those weren't your last hours." I scramble to my feet and pull my clothes on. "We have work to do and we're running out of time."

His eyes are soft and he looks sad. "You need to do what I asked you, Saffy."

I shake my head, stalking to Sylvia's bookcases. "I'm

going to search this room to find every spell that might help, and use them all on you."

"Our time's up." He picks up his clothes and starts putting them on. "You don't need to feel guilty. You've done everything you could."

"No, I haven't. I shouldn't have fallen asleep." Grabbing another grimoire from the shelf, I pull it down and open it roughly, scanning the pages.

He gestures around the room, to the bookcases that line all four walls. "You can't search every book in here."

"Watch me."

"It'd be nice if you could put your hand on the right book by chance, but it doesn't usually work that way."

The words ring in my ears, stirring a memory of a long-forgotten game I used to play with my mother. She used to be big on instinct, on letting her subconscious make decisions. She'd turn down random streets while she was driving, saying it just felt like the right way to go. She'd take us to places we'd never have seen otherwise.

When we got hopelessly lost, she'd make it into a game. She'd laugh as we drove, letting me pick which street to turn down next. My mother had the best laugh.

My breath catches in my throat. I've pushed all my memories away, shoved them down where they can't hurt. I squashed my longing for my lost magic into the same corner of my soul.

Now it's all coming out.

I take a deep breath, then close my eyes and turn slowly, letting my subconscious guide me. I hear my mother's laugh, and catch the smell of her perfume. My arm lifts of its own accord and I pull a tiny book out of the shelves.

It's a slim leather-bound volume with a swirling symbol on the front. The symbol seems to be moving at first and I have to narrow my eyes at it before the illusion fades away and it becomes just a pattern.

I open it to a random page. It seems to be a book of poetry, the last thing I'd expect to find amongst Sylvia's most dangerous grimoires.

I start reading the first lines of the poem printed there. *"Though she walked alone in milk-bathed moonlight…"*

That's as far as I get before the letters and words start moving, rearranging themselves on the page like they're dancing. A picture of a vine that was winding itself around the edges of the page dances too, the vines competing with the letters for space.

I've never seen anything like it.

Flicking through the pages, I try to read more poems, but the letters move too quickly. What kind of poetry book is this?

"Have you found something?" asks Xander.

"I'm not sure. But it's strange." I turn back to the first page, meaning to start from the beginning, and my own name jumps out at me. On the flyleaf is a dedication, the words written in ornate cursive letters.

This book is dedicated to Sapphira. Follow the strands, no matter how tangled, to the beginning of the skein.

"What the…?" I run my hand over the dedication, half expecting its letters to rearrange themselves into new words, but they're the only ones in this book that seem fixed in place.

"What's the matter?" Xander moves to stand next to me.

"Look."

He takes the book from me, and frowns. "Is it dedicated to you?"

"How can it be? Must be a different Sapphira. Or maybe the dedication changes to the name of whoever's reading it."

"I'm reading it, and it's not changing to my name."

I take the book back so I can flick through it, trying to work out what the dancing words say. On one of the last pages is a grainy, old-fashioned photograph of the author, and when I see it, I draw in a shocked breath.

"That's my cousin Sylvia," I tell Xander, showing him the photo. "It's so weird. She didn't write a book."

The woman's hair is long and lighter than Sylvia's, and pulled back into a loose bun, nothing like my cousin's bob. And now that I'm looking more closely, her face shape is a little different, her nose longer and her chin narrower.

Xander reads the inscription printed under the photo. "It says her name is Arabella Lightfoot."

"I guess it's not my cousin. But she's got to be related to Sylvia. She's the spitting image." My chest aches as I run my fingers over the photo. I wish Sylvia were still here. She loved books and could talk about them for hours, her eyes alight with enthusiasm.

Swallowing a surge of grief, I keep flipping the pages, turning them at random.

In the middle of the book, the vines around the edges of the page move together more purposefully to form an actual drawing. A jackal-headed monster. It turns its head and stares at me with dark, animal eyes. I jerk back with shock, almost dropping the book. *Jeqabeel?*

There are letters printed next to the picture, but they're dancing like the rest of the book, refusing to stay still long enough to form words. Maybe Sylvia's wards are blocking the magic.

"I need to take the book outside," I tell Xander. "If I give it power, it might tell us something useful."

"You think this book might hold the answer?" He

sounds so hopeful, my heart twists. He was pretending to be resigned to his fate, but now I know better.

"Only one way to find out. Stay here. I'll be back in a few minutes." I open the portal and push my way out of the athenaeum.

Syliva's living room is light, with early morning sunlight coming through the windows. Dammit, we must have slept all night.

Taking the book to the window, I glance again at the dedication before turning to its middle pages. Now the letters are ordering themselves, fitting themselves together to make words.

Jeqabeel is a powerful, immortal demon that cannot be destroyed.

My heart sinks. Aunt Therese already told me this, but now it's here in black and white. How the hell are we supposed to get rid of a demon that can't be destroyed?

The demon can be captured and confined.

At least that's better than nothing.

The demon will attempt to consume the vessel in which it's trapped.

Jeqabeel is consuming Xander. I already know that.

Somehow my ancestors managed to put the demon's essence into its own thigh bone, which was the perfect container for it—after all, it can't consume itself. But my magic turned the bone to dust.

Frantically, I flick through the rest of the book. It doesn't contain poems. Looking like a book of poetry must have been a protection mechanism. It's actually a spell book, but the spells seem ordinary. The only weird thing about it is that every spell book I've ever seen focuses on just one type of magic, but this one has spells for both animal and earth magic, as though it were written espe-cially for me.

But that's a crazy thought. It couldn't have been written for me.

Its spells aren't like any I've seen before. There's a disgusting-sounding one for melting flesh, one for using earth magic to harden and strengthen limbs, and another for softening stone to make it spongy.

There's also a cryptic one that doesn't seem to be either animal or earth magic. While most of the spells are written in plain black type, this one looks handwritten in a dark red ink that I have a feeling might be mixed with blood. It's called *Binde Magick*, and I think it's in archaic English.

I've never seen a spell that old. Is it a binding spell of some sort? If only I could read archaic English, maybe I'd be able to figure it out.

There's a publisher's address on the book's last page, and the date of publication, which is the year 1894. I blink with surprise. The book is over a hundred and twenty years old? It looks new.

This whole thing is getting stranger and stranger.

I read carefully through the dozen or so spells in the book, then re-read the information about Jeqabeel. None of it seems like it has the potential to help.

No, I can't accept that. There has to be something else here that I'm not seeing. Why else would this book be with all the dangerous grimoires that have to be locked up? Maybe the book needs something from me to release its secrets? If so, there's only one thing it could be waiting for.

Tucked into the back of Syliva's desk drawer, I find one of her small ceremonial knives. When I pick it up, I feel the shimmer of a spell on the knife. Most have a healing spell worked into them to heal the cut once the magic is done.

I put the open book on the desk and slice a small cut across the tip of my forefinger. The blood oozes up, forming a perfect sphere on the tip of my finger that transfixes me for a moment. Such a tiny, insignificant thing, and yet so vital to witches. I take a deep breath, then let my blood drip down onto the middle page of the spell book, the page with the information about Jeqabeel.

My magic surges.

Instead of landing on the page and staining it red, the drop of blood sinks into the book like it's a deep pool, and disappears. As soon as my blood is gone from sight, something knots tightly onto my magic, and I gasp at the uncomfortable sensation. Then the twisted strands of my magic flow out of my body and into the paper, turning silver the closer they get to the small grimoire, before disappearing inside.

I try to hold the strands in, pulling back on my magic, but it's impossible to control.

The book is sucking me dry of magic, and there's nothing I can do to stop it.

Panic fills me, my blood pounding in my ears as I try to break the connection. I fight to take a step back, or turn away, but I can't move. My feet are frozen in place. There's no way to escape the unrelenting pull of the book.

If I can't step away, what if I push the book away instead? I thrust out my hand, but as soon as I touch the open page of the small grimoire, its pages become soft and pliant, like the mortar I use on my stone walls. My fingers sink into it, their tips disappearing.

I try to yank my hand away again, but it's stuck. Caught inside the pages.

I drag in a shocked breath. I've made things worse, not better.

My magic is all but depleted, and no matter how hard I pull, I can't tug my fingers from the book. I struggle to breathe in the suddenly thick air around me. Tiny stars dance in front of my eyes.

As the last of my magic drains, I'm sure the book will let me go. Then my arm starts prickling and a new sensation grows.

The magic is no longer flowing out of me into the book. It's reversed direction. Strands of pale, luminescent magic emerge from the pages and curl up my arm. The book's magic fills me up like a river flooding a valley.

My hand sinks further into the book, but now it's me that's deepening the connection. I can't help it. The magic fills me with energy, my blood fizzing with power. It feels like nothing I've ever experienced.

The spells that were inside the book detach from its pages. The words and runes seep out of the book, march along my wrist and up my arm. They swarm into me like a moving tattoo, writing themselves into my skin.

One by one, all the spells work their way inside me, imprinting themselves through my flesh, burning themselves into my memory, until they sink below the surface and embed themselves deep inside me, invisible once more.

I feel completely full, like every crevice of my body has expanded and taken on more than it should have. I can't move, I can't think. I can't see the words any more, but I can feel them inside me. I know every word that wrote itself on my flesh, intimately and perfectly.

When the book is empty, I pull my hand back out of it. Its blank, empty pages flutter.

I don't know what to think. Most witches take years to learn the bare minimum of runes and words to focus their magic for different spells. It's an evolving, laborious process that goes on for most of their lives. Being able to simply absorb a spell and recall every word isn't possible.

And yet, I can picture the rune for each spell I absorbed, and recite what the spell does, as though I'd learned it by heart.

I close my eyes, sorting through the spells in my mind. It feels weirdly like leafing through the book. Surely other witches must have discovered how to do this before? I can't be the only person who's ever absorbed spells without having to learn them.

Unless it was the weird spell in the book that allowed me to take them in. *Binde Magick.* Could it have been a spell to bind the book's spells inside me?

If that was what the spell was for, why don't other witches use it all the—?

A scraping noise comes from the kitchen.

I spin around, all my muscles tense. What was that? Is somebody else here?

Heart beating fast, I stay frozen for several minutes, listening hard. Maybe I imagined it. Perhaps it was just—

A loud bang comes from beyond the open door, like a cupboard door slamming.

Who could be there? The Unseen? Dallas? Magnus come to get Xander?

Creeping forward, I peer around the kitchen door.

Chapter Eighteen

A large form is crouched on the floor, making chomping noises.

My already suffering heart stops for a beat before I realize who—what—it is.

Ratticus.

Sylvia's giant rat is in her kitchen, sitting up on his hindquarters. He's holding a box of cookies with one hand and eating one of the cookies with the other.

I let out my breath, putting my hand on my heart to calm its wild thumping. "Ratticus," I say. "How did you get in here?"

He blinks at me. "Here." His squeaky, high-pitched voice seems much too reedy for his Labrador-sized body.

It makes sense that Ratticus would come back to Sylvia's. It's his home, after all. The place he knows best.

"That was clever of you to break in here, Ratticus." I walk up to him and pat his head while he eats. "Can't be easy for a rat your size to get inside. I'm glad you're okay."

"Okay." He swallows the last of the cookie, then pulls

another out of the box. It's a disturbingly human way to eat. Not rat-like in the slightest.

But any weirdness is not his fault. I'm the one who changed him, and I feel awful that with everything that's been going on I'd pushed him out of my mind and left him to fend for himself.

"A rat your size must need a lot of food to keep full, I guess. Let me check the cupboards and see if I can find something else for you to eat."

Sylvia's kitchen is still full of food, and I guess one day I'll have to come and clean it out. But at least it means there's plenty to choose from for Ratticus. I tip an assortment of tinned meats and vegetables onto Sylvia's biggest dinner plate, and watch him eat delicately with his hands.

Seeing as the last thing I ate was yesterday's waffles, I should be hungry too. But nerves have compressed my stomach into a small, hard ball, and the last thing I feel like is food.

"How many words can you say?" I ask Ratticus curiously.

He looks at me with his mouth full, and chews, not saying anything.

"The strong, silent type, huh?" I nod. "That's fine by me. But I bet you want to go back to normal size, right? To the way you were?"

Theoretically, I should be able to untangle the magic that transformed him, returning him back to his original state.

But what about the gargoyle's tail? And the feathers I left on Agnes's neck and arms when I changed her back from being a chicken? After sleeping, my magic is back to its full power, which means it'll be almost impossible to control. I don't want to make things even worse for Ratticus by giving him extra appendages by mistake.

If I use a spell to help focus my animal magic, maybe it'll help. But none of the spells I absorbed from the weird little spell book are designed to turn magically-mutated creatures back into their original form.

Sylvia's house is full of books. All her most powerful grimoires are in her athenaeum, but there are plenty of ordinary spell books in the bookcases that line the living room. After running one finger along their spines, I find a few that deal with animal magic. And a quick scan of each book's table of contents delivers what I'm after. A reversal spell for magic that's gone wrong.

I'm about to prick my already-healed finger to try it, when I hesitate. Instead of trying to copy the complicated rune from the book, and probably losing control of my magic in the meantime, can I absorb the spell?

I take a deep breath and press the knife into my skin. As a drop of blood appears and my magic surges, I reach inside myself for the mysterious spell I absorbed. *Binde Magick*. Then I press my bloody finger onto the page of the animal magic spell book.

The *Binde Magick* rune appears on the inside of my forearm like a tattoo, coming up through my flesh as I summon it into being. My hand sinks deeply into the paper, and all the animal magic spells in the book march off the page and onto my skin, until long lines of writing are coursing up my arm. I can feel them sinking into me, settling deep inside.

It's intoxicating.

When the pages are empty, I drop the book. Its knowledge fills me, and its spells are now mine to use. What a rush. If I had time, I'd do the same thing to every spell book on Sylvia's bookshelf, and drag every spell I could ever need into me, ready to use.

The way the rune appeared on my skin without me

having to remember it and draw it on? I've never heard of anybody being able to do that. But it felt so effortless.

The only problem is, I don't know if the spells I'm taking in are going to be strong enough to control my violent magic. They're designed for regular witches with just one kind of magic, not my double-strength, chaotic version.

There's only one way to find out.

I turn to Ratticus, who's still working his way through the plate of food I gave him. "Are you ready to give one of the spells a try?" My voice comes out a little shaky from the rush that absorbing all the magical spells gave me.

I should probably be more nervous about experimenting on a living creature. The last thing I want is to accidentally hurt Ratticus. But I'm so full of spells, I'm like a kid with a new bike. If I don't try using them, I'll burst.

Ratticus's whiskers twitch. "Try," he says.

I narrow my eyes at him. "Do you understand what I'm asking, or are you just repeating the last word I say?"

"Say."

I guess that answers my question, but I keep talking anyway, in case he can understand me. "I'm going to try turning you back to your normal size now."

Ratticus makes a snorting sound. I'm not sure if he's choking on his food, or he's afraid I'm going to hurt him. Maybe both.

"Are you ready?" I ask with Sylvia's knife poised over my hand. "If you don't want me to do this, tell me now, okay?"

"Okay," he says.

I'm already slicing the knife into my finger.

My magic surges, as strong and impossible to control as ever. But I find the right spell easily, and its rune emerges from inside me, drawing itself onto the inside of my forearm.

As my magic pours out of me, I can see the tangled strands that hold Ratticus's transformation in place. It's mostly animal magic, but the earth magic distorts it, snarling it into a confusion of twisting strands that look impossible to untangle.

My animal and earth magic are usually fused together in a violent mess, both looking for an outlet. This time, it feels different. The rune on my arm helps me focus the animal magic. It's like a funnel that draws in the swirling mess and tightens it into a single thread that's far easier to control.

But the rune on my arm bulges under the pressure, my flesh distorting as it strains to contain such powerful magic.

It hurts. I cry out in pain as the rune seems to expand beyond the limits of where my flesh should be able to go. The power is pushing it out too far, stretching my muscles and tendons beyond their endurance.

Fighting through the pain, I channel the animal magic to Ratticus. The rune helps me control the magic, holding enough of it back so I can use it to help me unpick what's already there. My animal magic unravels the old strands, pulling them apart and tearing away Ratticus's transformation, undoing the previous spell.

As the magic pours into Ratticus, the pressure on my arm increases and the pain becomes unbearable. Ratticus is shrinking, returning to his normal size. I grit my teeth and clench my fists. I have to keep going. It's working. I can't stop, no matter how much it hurts.

Then I feel my earth magic. It's searching for its own outlet, and it's being drawn to something powerful. It's heading toward… No!

Before I can stop it, my earth magic slams into the

wards that protect Sylvia's house, shattering them into pieces.

The rune on my arm expands past the limits of my flesh, and I feel my skin tear. I scream with pain, pulling the small amount of animal magic I have left back inside myself.

My legs are too weak to support me, so I sink onto Sylvia's kitchen floor. I'm gasping for breath, and my chest is heaving. My arm should be torn apart. It's not. My skin is unbroken. I don't have so much as a red mark to show where the flesh strained and tore.

All I can think of is Xander. Is he okay? The wards in Sylvia's athenaeum should still be protecting him, keeping the demon at bay. But I need to check on him, to make sure.

At least Ratticus is back to the size he used to be, looking the way he always did. A normal black rat again. Whiskers twitching, he sniffs at the small amount of food left on the plate I gave him. He seems completely unconcerned by the violence of the magic I used to transform him back to his old self.

"At least I didn't hurt you," I pant, still breathless. "Didn't feel a thing, did you Ratticus?"

He sits back on his hind legs and lifts his head. His beady eyes can't possibly narrow, can they? It looks like he's glaring at me.

"Actually, it stung like a bitch," says a reedy, petulant voice inside my head.

I freeze, mid-pant. "What?" My voice comes out even squeakier than his. "What did you say?"

Then I hear the front door of Sylvia's house open. Footsteps tell me somebody's coming inside.

Ratticus runs to my leg and scrambles up my clothes, pulling himself up my torso and onto my shoulder. He nestles into my neck like he's done a million times before. Only this time feels different. Did I really hear him speak inside my head or did I just imagine it?

No time to figure it out either way. With Ratticus mostly hidden in my hair, I scramble to my feet and grab the biggest kitchen knife I can find.

Then I ease into the hall.

There's a figure standing at the open doorway, outlined by the light from outside.

It's the Veritas. She's wearing a white dress, and I'm struck again by how young she is, only about thirteen. Her dark eyes burn from her pale face.

"It's time, Saffy. You and Xander must come with me," she lisps.

For a moment, I panic. I need more time.

Then I feel a tingle over my body, and a strong sense of being pulled. It's like when the Unseen controlled me, but it doesn't feel quite so creepy, and so far at least, it doesn't hurt. It must be the spell Magnus placed on me to call me back to the council chambers.

"Xander's inside the athenaeum." I tell the Veritas. "The wards stop the demon from taking over. If he comes out here, it'll be in charge again."

She nods. "That's why I'm here, so I can control him and take him safely to the council chambers."

My mind racing, I pick up the blank book that was written by Arabella Lightfoot. There's no use trying to run. The Veritas is powerful, and I have no idea how I could get Xander safely away from her. And with Magnus's spell to fight, I wouldn't stand a chance.

The Veritas follows and puts her small hand on my arm. She stares intently at me, like she knows I'm trying to figure out a way to escape.

"You must accept it," she says. "You can't resist our

power." Energy tingles along my skin, clamping down over my magic. Her magic glows pure white.

My heart sinks. She's right. There's no way I can fight it.

"*Face it*," Ratticus says in my head. "*You're screwed.*"

Chapter Nineteen

The rest of the Blood Council are in the council chambers, an enormous room with a round skylight set into the high ceiling. This is where the council meet to create spells strong enough to rule the entire witch community. I'm part of that too, however reluctantly. I can feel the shared bond of the council magic inside me.

The morning sun is shining through the skylight, filtering down in finger-of-god shafts that highlight the witches waiting for us.

They're here to pronounce sentence on Xander.

Dallas is standing in one of the nine circles carved into the floor, and he doesn't bother to disguise the hate that blazes in his eyes. He's long-limbed, and looks more gaunt than ever. Dark shadows are carved into his deathly white cheeks, and his black suit hangs limply over his body, like it would over a skeleton.

Magnus is there too, apparently none the worse for his gunshot wound. His long gray beard hangs half-way down the front of his shirt, and his eyes are creased as though he's nursing deep worries.

The Veritas steps into one of the circles and folds her hands together in front of her. She clearly has a thing for white dresses, because they're all she ever seems to wear.

In another circle is a witch I don't know. I saw her the last time I was here, when I killed Uncle Ray and sent the demon into Xander. Not a night that ranks high on my list of great memories.

The five of us are all that's left of the council. Do the rest of the witch community know how seriously depleted the Blood Council is?

I deliberately don't stand in one of the circles, but stop in front of Magnus with Xander beside me. His eyes are glowing red, but he can't speak. The council members have shackled and gagged him using just their magic. That same magic makes the air in the chamber thick with energy, like breathing in flames.

I'm carrying the small spell book I absorbed, and have Ratticus nestled in the curve of my neck, his small black body mostly hidden by my hair. His sharp little claws dig into my skin. "*The old man smells like a dog,*" he complains in my head. "*I hate dogs.*"

"Sapphira, it's time to do our duty." Magnus at least looks sad about it. His eyes are soft and his tone is regretful.

I shake my head. "Turning Xander into stone won't help. The demon will consume any vessel that holds it. That means it'll take over Xander anyway. Our only chance is to get the demon out of Xander and into something it *can't* consume."

"How do you know?"

I thrust out the spell book. "This was dedicated to me, and talked about Jeqabeel. And the woman who wrote it looked exactly like Sylvia. It's too much of a coincidence not to be important."

Magnus takes the book and flips through it, his brow furrowed. "Its pages are blank."

"Because I absorbed everything that was in it."

He shakes his head, looking at me warily, as though I might be unstable. "You absorbed it?"

"Its spells are inside me now. I absorbed them right out of the pages."

"That's not possible."

"I'll prove it. Give me a knife and I'll use one of them."

He offers me a small smile. "Nice try, Sapphira. But we can't allow you to use your magic, and even if you did, you can't stop what we need to do." His voice is deceptively kind. "You're tired and upset. I understand, Saffy. This isn't easy for any of us. We don't do this lightly."

"But—"

"Must we listen to her nonsense?" snarls Dallas. He gestures at Xander, who's standing obediently in front of the council although the demon inside him must be seething. "We all know she'll say anything to protect her precious mundane. We should bind her mouth to keep her quiet."

"*Friend of yours?*" asks Ratticus in my head. "*Didn't know you were so popular.*"

I ignore both Dallas and the rat, keeping my gaze fixed on Magnus. "Why not just keep Xander under your control instead of turning him to stone? Aunt Therese said—"

"I've had enough of the way you pander to her, Magnus." Dallas waves an impatient hand, brushing my objections away. "We know what we need to do. Let's stop wasting time and get it done. We have other things we need to discuss, like how we're going to deal with the

Unseen and his dark magic. I told Therese she'd regret defending him all these years."

Magnus nods and pulls a ceremonial knife from a pocket in his robe. "I'm sorry, Sapphira, but Dallas is right. It's time to do our duty."

"Xander, step forward," lisps the Veritas, her eyes turning pure white.

Xander obeys, though his face twists into an ugly scowl.

"Stop!" I move between him and Magnus. "Aunt Therese said you could sedate him while we find a way to get the demon out of him."

"She was too soft," snaps Dallas. "Always trying to make people feel better." He grimaces as though the idea gives him a bad taste in his mouth.

My fists clench as I fight an overwhelming urge to take a swing at Dallas.

"Therese's death was a terrible shock for all of us." Magnus presses his lips together, and the lines in his face deepen as he shoots Dallas a glare. He looks as though my aunt's death has hit him hard. "But Therese was committed to the council, and she respected our laws. I've made my decision and it will be obeyed." He clamps his hand on my shoulder and I feel the shared magic of the council come to life inside me. It's back to full strength after Aunt Therese all but depleted it. Now Magnus is drawing on it, and its power is fierce.

Suddenly, my limbs aren't my own. My feet move of their own accord, walking to one of the dark circles etched into the floor.

Ratticus moves on my shoulder, his sharp claws digging deeper into my skin. *"Are you going to roll over and let them rub your belly?"*

His voice in my head gives me the strength to close my

eyes and fight the power of the council. I refuse to let them get their way, especially if they think they're going to make me part of this. There's no way I'm going to help them turn Xander to stone. They'll have to kill me first.

By sheer force of will, I make my feet stop moving.

For just a second.

Then they move again, and there's not a thing I can do to stop them. They carry me into the circle, then stop of their own accord, holding me in place.

The Veritas's white magic curls from her small body, glowing strands that stretch toward Xander.

I can't prevent this from happening. I can't even lift a finger.

All four council members start chanting. Low, mesmerising words that make me feel like I'm floating through a murky fog. The Blood Council magic inside me connects to them, and my mouth opens of its own accord. I hear the chant coming from my own throat. No matter how hard I try, I can't keep myself from helping the council cast the spell that's going to turn Xander into a statue.

The Veritas's magic surrounds Xander, covering him with a white glow.

The chanting gets louder. It fills my head until it's all I can hear, and still my own mouth keeps moving. The chant pours from my mouth, the sound mingling with the others as though we share a single voice.

"*Nice singing*," says Ratticus in my head. "*Your friends really know how to party.*"

My voice softens as I fight the compulsion to chant with everything I've got. Can I stop the spell? Can I—?

An explosion blasts the room apart.

I'm flung sideways. Ratticus squeaks as he flies off my shoulder. My back slams into the wall, then I land hard on the floor. Chunks of stone rain down around me, and so much dirt swirls, I can't see a thing.

Did the room just explode? Where's Xander?

Dragging in a lungful of stone dust, I cough and splutter, then try pushing myself to my feet. My body aches, but I don't seem to have broken any bones. I have no idea if Ratticus survived the blast.

Through the dust, the Unseen strides toward me. He's drawn runes on his face, and the blood has dripped down his neck to stain the collar of his open brown overcoat and his filthy old-man's shirt. His shirt is unbuttoned at the top, giving me a tantalizing glimpse of my mother's ring dangling from his necklace. And where bare skin is revealed, the Unseen's body gleams faintly red, like he's radioactive and emitting light.

The Unseen stops in front of a figure that's standing erect, seemingly unaffected by the explosion. *Xander.* Relief floods through me. At least he's still alive and hasn't been turned to stone. If only his eyes weren't redder than ever.

The Unseen bows to him. "My lord."

The rest of the witches are strewn about in the rubble and debris. They pull themselves slowly to their feet, hacking and coughing like I am.

Ignoring them, Xander focuses on the Unseen. "I shall reward you," he drawls.

The Unseen bows again, then gives his creepy, sharpened-teeth smile. "It wasn't difficult to overcome them. They're weak, and so few in number."

The witch I don't know staggers toward him, the quickest to recover from the explosion. She pulls a small glass bottle from the pocket of her dress and throws it at the Unseen's feet, where it smashes into pieces. Acid-green smoke rises from the smashed pieces, but the Unseen mutters a few words and motions with one glowing hand, waving it away as though it's nothing.

"Your potions don't work on me." The Unseen tugs a long-bladed knife from his coat. Moving faster than an old man should be able to, he plunges the knife into the witch's chest.

It happens so quickly, she doesn't have time to move away. She doesn't make a sound, not a scream or even a gasp. She just crumples to the ground.

Pain and anguish fill me as the link inside me reacts to the life draining from her body.

The Unseen bends and places the fingertips of one hand over the wound. He murmurs an incantation, and her body starts to jerk and rock. For a split second, I think he's going to repair the damage and keep her from dying, and my heart leaps in my chest.

But of course, that's not what he's doing.

Her green-tinged magic flows up the Unseen's fingers, over his hands and into his arms, before being absorbed into his skin. The faint light that was shining from him gets brighter. The hairs on my arms stand on end, and I can feel his power building. As the witch dies, the Unseen draws her power into himself.

I have to stop him.

Magnus and Dallas have the same idea as I do, and they both start forward too. But the Unseen throws up a hand and we run up against a red, seething barrier of magic.

The witch dies. I feel the moment of her death as a sharp pain, deep in my gut. Her council bond breaks as soon as her heart stops beating, and we're even fewer than before. Even weaker.

The Veritas lets out a moan. Her young face is filled with so much pain and loss that I can't bear it. The Unseen doesn't care how many people he hurts, and Jeqabeel's taking pleasure in it. Xander wears a smile even more horrible than the Unseen's.

Anger wells up inside me. Not just anger, but a burning, uncontrollable rage.

"I'm going to kill you!" I don't even realise I've yelled until I hear the words leave my mouth.

The demon glares at me through Xander's eyes. "You've been nothing but trouble," he spits. "I'm going to watch you die, painfully and slowly for a very long time. You'll scream for mercy until your throat bleeds and you can scream no more."

The Unseen turns his gaze onto me. His eyes glitter and his expression makes me shiver. "I've already made arrangements for Sapphira to be part of our ceremony, my lord, so you'll get your wish."

My body goes cold as a rush of fear dulls my rage. "What's that supposed to mean?"

The Unseen beckons to me. "If you want to save the rest of the council, you'll come with us. Otherwise I will destroy them all, as easily as I did her." He flicks his hand dismissively to where the dead witch lies crumpled on the floor beside him. With the extra magic he's absorbed, he's stronger than ever, his power glowing brighter.

I glance over at Magnus, Dallas and the Veritas. Right now, they're as weak as I am, and I have no doubt the Unseen could make good on his threat.

"Enough talk," growls Xander. "I need to be free of this body." He strides to where the room's enormous oak doors used to be, before the Unseen blasted them into shards.

Before I can move, Magnus flings a hailstorm of ice bullets at the Unseen. At the same time, Dallas launches a tornado that whips toward him. White strands of magic extend from the Veritas.

If I had a knife I'd use it, but all I have are my own fingernails. I scratch at one of the most recent cuts I made in my palm, digging my woefully short, ripped nails into the wound. A tiny dot of red appears, barely any blood managing to break through. Before I can use my magic to help the others, it needs more blood.

As I'm trying to deepen the cut, the dark witch lifts his hands and the room darkens. Both ice and wind vaporise into nothing. The bloody runes on the Unseen's face glow, and a swirling ball of red energy forms between his fingers, growing fast, until it's so large, bright, and hot, I can barely see the witch who wields it.

He flings it toward Magnus and Dallas, who dive for the ground. The ball explodes against the wall behind them, tearing a hole right through it. Magnus howls in pain, and the Veritas screams, covering her head. The blast of heat sears my face, so I can imagine how much worse it must be for the others. I'm surprised their clothes aren't alight.

"*Too hot,*" squeaks Ratticus in my mind. "*Make him stop.*" I spot the rat running from the rubble, tucking his small body under a stone near my foot.

"That's enough!" I yell at the Unseen. "Don't hurt them." Too many people have already died. I can't bear to watch him kill anyone else.

The Unseen turns to me. "You know what you have to do. Come with us."

"All right," I snarl. "Promise to leave them unhurt, and I will." Hopefully he believes me. The instant he lets his guard down, I'm going to throw all the magic I've got at him.

"You have something of mine." The Unseen holds his

hand up, displaying his shortened pinky finger. "Give it back."

Shoving my hand in my pocket, I touch the small wrapped bundle Aunt Therese gave me, reassuring myself that it's still safe. Giving it to him would be signing my death warrant.

Stepping back, I shake my head. "No way. That's not part of the deal."

"Let me tell you what the deal is, Sapphira. You'll do everything I command, or I'll kill your friends on the council, then force you to do what I want."

If glares could kill, the look I'm giving him would burn all the flesh from his body. "Leave them alone. I'll go with you, but I'm keeping your creepy finger bone."

The Unseen flashes me his butt-ugly smile. He lifts one hand, and I feel energy crackle, like lightning on a hot, sticky evening. Red strands of magic ooze over his skin, thick and rich as congealing blood. The strength of his power, the threat of it, makes all my hair stand on end.

He's going to try to use his magic to take the bone. I can't let him do that.

Desperately, I dig my fingernails into the cut on my palm, trying to make more blood well. At the same time, I reach inside me for the worst spell I can—

"Look out," shouts Magnus.

Rough arms wrap around me from behind. A large body envelopes me, Xander's arms rippling with muscles and so achingly familiar that for a split second my heart leaps.

Then pain lights up my skin.

At the same time, a horrible voice worms into my brain, its words eating into my skull like putrid maggots. *"You'll beg me for death. I'll relish your sobs and drink down your sweet agony. Your screams will—"*

With all my strength, I slam my elbow backward into Xander's stomach, wrenching myself free, then spinning to face him.

He stands straight, not bent over, in spite of the fact I just buried my elbow in his gut. There's no pain on his face. He doesn't even look winded. Instead he gives me a triumphant smile.

In his hand is a small package wrapped in tissue paper. The pain I got from touching him is fading, but as I stare at the package, cold fear rushes to take its place.

It's the finger bone. Xander snatched it from my pocket.

A tingling sensation ripples through me, and I can taste something horrible and metallic in the back of my throat. The Unseen's power feels slimy. Invasive. Thanks to my mother's ring, he can control me again.

The Unseen goes to Xander and takes the bone from him. He holds it up, smirking, and it erupts into flames. His hand burns so fiercely, I flinch backward, shielding my face from the blaze.

The bone burns until there's nothing left of it.

I'm expecting the flames to die then, but they don't. Instead the Unseen flattens his palm and creates an enormous fireball. A fireball with a black core instead of a red one, just like the one he used to kill Aunt Therese.

My heart stops.

He turns to the three remaining council members. Dallas, Magnus, and the Veritas are cowering against the wall. They're unprotected.

He's going to kill them.

"No!" I yell. "You promised you wouldn't hurt them if I went with you."

The Unseen doesn't glance in my direction, but his power wraps more tightly around me, crushing my chest, making it hard to breathe. I can't move, can't lift a hand or even turn my head.

The last remaining council members will die in front of my eyes and I can't do anything to help them.

The three of them move so they're standing shoulder to shoulder, just as the Unseen launches his fireball. I feel the draw of their shared magic, and a shimmering shield comes up in front of them. The fireball hits the shield.

The heat is so intense, my flesh feels like it's searing. I can't stagger backward, or raise my hands to protect myself. The fireball burns hot and bright, then it goes out. Behind it is nothing.

The council members are gone.

My heart clenches. Then I realize they must have escaped through the hole in the wall. Otherwise, I would have felt them die.

Ratticus scuttles out from his hiding place near the blast zone. "*He's trying to fry me,*" he squeaks into my head. "*I told you to do something.*" He runs up my clothes and buries himself under my T-shirt. When he's dug himself painfully into the curve of my collarbone, he gives me a sharp nip for good measure. With the Unseen's magic holding me frozen, I can't even wince.

The Unseen turns to Xander. "My lord, I can follow and kill them."

Xander shakes his head. "First, I must escape this body. It feels dead. A prison of meat." He shudders.

"Of course. I have everything we'll need for the cere-mony waiting at my home." The Unseen motions to me, and my feet follow him without my permission.

"I'm going to kill you," I promise as I march obediently behind him out of the council chambers.

"*Believe it when I see it,*" Ratticus mutters into my head.

Chapter Twenty

As I reluctantly walk down the steps to the Unseen's basement for the third time, I wish history would stop repeating itself. I never wanted to see—or smell—this stinking place again.

Ratticus is still and silent, nestled under my hair. He's so quiet, I think he must be in shock. If the demon or the Unseen know he's there, neither of them care.

The Unseen strides to his spell-casting table, Xander beside him. The eight-legged statue in the corner is as hideous as ever, and the power of the grimoires on the Unseen's enormous bookshelves sends shivers down my spine. *Dark magic grimoires.* They're probably full of spells designed to inflict pain and suffering. Spells that need other peoples' blood to use them. Dark magic may be powerful, but there's a good reason that using it is punishable by death.

The two worst grimoires are open on the Unseen's table. Their pages vibrate with dark power, and they give off a nasty, prickling energy that makes me want to keep as much distance as I can.

There's a strange stench in the Unseen's dungeon, even worse than when I've been here before. It's not the rotting smell of the Unseen's mouth, and it's stronger than the stink of dampness and mould. This smell is something different.

It's burning hair.

A whimpering noise comes from behind the Unseen's spell table. The Unseen looks down at something I can't see, and his smile is smug. It's the smile of someone who likes torturing kittens. I'm absolutely certain I don't want to see what put that smile on his face.

"I have a gift for you, Sapphira." When the Unseen gestures, I'm forced to move closer, to where I can see what's on the floor.

There's a person curled up, as small as she can get.

Jess.

Her wrists and ankles are tied, and she's gagged. Her blonde hair is matted with ash and blood, and blood is smeared on her pale face. She stares at me, her eyes wide with shock and fear.

I'm horrified at how she looks, but I'm also relieved beyond words to find her still alive. With the council so focused on the demon, I doubt they were even looking for her. I've been terrified the Unseen might have murdered her.

I try to rush to her, but can't step forward. "What have you done?" I growl at the Unseen. "Get away from her! Let her go!"

"I discovered her secret. Like me, she was hidden in plain sight. Magnus must have thought he was clever, keeping her tucked away like that. But now I've found her."

"Leave her out of this." I can't even clench my fists. "This is between you and me."

He smirks. "There's nothing between you and me, Sapphira. You mean nothing to me, except as a means to get what I want."

"I'll do anything you want if you let her go." It's a rash promise, but I don't care. Seeing Jess like this is one of the worst things I can imagine.

"You'll do what I command whether she's here or not." He puts one hand under Jess's arm and drags her onto a chair. Then he lashes her onto it with a length of rope, binding it so tightly around her that the rope digs into her flesh.

"What have you done to her?" I stare with horror at the shallow cuts on Jess's arms. "Have you been *torturing* her?"

"I wanted a little blood. Just a taste. But I've been waiting for you before starting on the main course."

"This guy's a piece of work." Ratticus is so scared, he's trembling against my neck. *"We need to leave now."*

If only.

I can't even reach up to reassure Ratticus. Instead I strain every muscle, trying with all my strength to break free of the spell that keeps me frozen. The Unseen ignores me, turning instead to a bowl of blood on the table.

"You have the power to give me corporal form?" demands Xander.

The Unseen inclines his head. "I've searched the grimoires and found a spell that will work. I've gathered sufficient blood from witches of each of the nine powers, and I will draw on the power of the Blood Council through Sapphira." His eyes glint over at me. "That was an unexpected boon."

Nine powers? There are only eight, everyone knows that.

Except there's the mysterious ninth circle in the council

chambers that's bugged me since I first saw it. What does the Unseen know that I don't?

The Unseen puts his hand on Jess's forehead, pushing her face back so she's forced to look up at Xander. "In addition, Sapphira's affection for this girl means her suffering will cause agony for both of them. The spell to create your corporeal body will be seasoned with their pain, making it even more powerful. We cannot fail."

Xander curls his lips in a feral snarl. "The last witch who tried was unable to finish the spell. This time, there must be no mistakes."

"I've been practising dark magic for many more years than Raymond. My power is far stronger than his ever was."

"Don't fail me," drawls Xander.

Jess's eyes are wide with terror, and her face is deathly pale. The Unseen bends down, bringing his ugly face near hers, and tugs off her gag. "Say hello to your friend," he commands.

Jess opens and closes her mouth a few times, working out the stiffness in her jaw. Then she clears her throat. But instead of saying anything, she spits at the Unseen. Her saliva sprays over his face, a big gob landing on his cheek.

"Say hello to my spit, you piece of shit," she snarls.

That's the Jess I know. I want to cheer, but I also want to tell her not to defy him. If she makes him angry, he'll just get more vicious.

Sure enough, the expression on the Unseen's face makes my gut clench.

"Don't hurt her," I snarl. "Don't you dare hurt her."

The Unseen lifts one hand and fire bursts from the tips of his fingers. His fingers glow hot, so bright they burn my eyes. He reaches out and clamps his hand around her arm, and the sizzling smell of burning flesh fills the small space. Jess screams.

"Stop!" I try frantically to struggle. "Stop it now!"

Ratticus lets out a frightened squeak and jumps off my shoulder, launching himself like a cowardly rat missile into the darkest corner of the room. He disappears behind a bookcase.

"Do something," I yell at him. "Help Jess!" I don't know what a rat could possibly do, but I'm desperate.

"*I'm hiding,*" he squeaks in my head. "*You help her.*"

The Unseen pulls his hand away and grins at Xander. "Their blood is going to be so sweet and full of pain. I can already taste it."

He bends down to smirk into Jess's face, and his necklace dangles out of the dirty, old-man's shirt he's wearing. My mother's ring is hanging off it, swinging tantalisingly in front of her. I've worn that ring every day for years, so if Jess sees it, she's sure to recognise it. Maybe she'll figure out that because he has it, I can't make a move to help her.

It's a long shot. I can't tell her about the ring without warning the Unseen. I can't even point at the damn thing. And with her hands tied, what would she do about it anyway?

"She's ready," purrs the Unseen. "Her blood is rich and saturated with agony."

Xander claps his hands together. "Then let's begin."

Chapter Twenty-One

Jess's wrists are bound together and her torso is lashed to the chair, but the Unseen yanks at one of her hands, forcing it open, then slices his knife across her palm. Bile rises in my throat as Jess moans with pain. I strain against the spell holding me in place, my muscles groaning with the effort, but it's no good.

He drips her blood into an ornately decorated metal goblet, until he has a substantial amount of thick red liquid. Then he looks at me. "Your turn." His eyes glitter as he walks toward me with the knife and goblet.

Xander steps toward me as well, moving to my other side. For once, I don't like having his bulk next to me. He leans close enough that his breath gusts across my cheek.

"Your fear is strong," he whispers. "It burns bright and hot, and so, so magical. It almost makes me want to make a home inside you, instead of my own true form."

"I'd fight you every step of the way," I grind out between gritted teeth. But I can't help my fear, and his nostrils flare as he drinks it in.

The Unseen holds his knife up in front of me. "Give me your hand," he orders.

I struggle with every inch of my being to disobey his request. But I can't, and my hand rises.

"Palm up."

I flip my hand over, and the Unseen holds the knife over it. He pauses to look me in the eyes, and I try to understand what Aunt Therese ever saw in him. She said he used to be a good person, but that doesn't seem possible. If he was once good, then this is what using dark magic has done to him. It's turned him into a monster.

My disgust must show on my face, because he snarls at me, his sharpened teeth bared.

"I control you, Saffy." He runs the knife over my palm and pain flares. "And now you'll give me what I want."

My magic surges, strong and urgent, but the blanket of control he's covered me with keeps it inside. Though it batters against his barrier, it's as trapped as I am.

This knife isn't like most ceremonial knives that have healing spells embedded in their blades. The pain stays with me, and the wound stays open as my blood flows and my magic fights more urgently to get out.

The Unseen pushes one finger into the wound, deliberately making it hurt more. I suck in a sharp breath, but clamp my teeth together, refusing to cry out. I won't give him that pleasure.

He takes his blood-covered finger, lifts it to my neck and draws a rune on my skin. I can't see what it is, but I feel the effects straight away. The magic from the bond I share with the rest of the Blood Council stirs. It's an immense amount of power that's been inert inside me, but now it uncurls.

My own magic still can't escape, but the council magic starts to flow slowly, as if being pulled out of me through a small funnel. It drains out with my blood into the goblet.

My blood starts to glow and sparkle with a silver light. Somehow, the Unseen has trapped the council's magic in my blood.

I try frantically to pull the magic back inside me, to deny it to him. But the Unseen's spell is too strong. The glass is filling, the blood sparkling brighter and brighter. I can't stop it. All I can do is scream soundlessly as it drains out of me.

He tips my palm, dripping the remaining blood from the knife wound into his goblet. He swirls the cup like it's a glass of fine wine, mixing my blood with Jess's. As the two merge, searing pain slices through my body. If I could, I'd drop to my knees.

Beside me, Xander makes a noise in the back of his throat. His eyes are glowing and he licks his lips, visibly excited by my torment. I wish I could shove all my pain and suffering down inside me, to deny it to the demon. But Jeqabeel can clearly feel it and is drinking down every morsel.

When he's finished bleeding me and the council's power is depleted, the Unseen waves a hand. "Sit on the ground," he orders. My legs go out from under me, and I sit on the basement's stone floor.

The Unseen hands the goblet to Xander who gulps down the blood. When he lowers it, his mouth is ringed with red. He throws his head back and gives a triumphant roar. "More!" He bangs the goblet down on the spell table. "Give me more!"

The Unseen turns to Jess, who cowers back. He leans down, reaching for her hand, eager to take more blood. Jess makes a guttural sound, like it's the last straw. She cranes forward and bites the ring on the necklace dangling near her face. When she yanks her head back, the chain snaps. The Unseen howls in anger, but it's too late.

Jess spits my grandmother's ring onto the ground in my direction. For a second, our eyes meet. The breath leaves my lungs.

She recognized the ring.

The magic that was holding me frozen falls away. Without hesitation, I scramble to the ring and snatch it off the floor with my blood-soaked hand. The cut on my palm is still flowing and my own special double-whammy of magic surges. The ring glows red-hot in my palm before I manage to shove it on my finger.

Twisting together, my animal and earth magic try to explode out of me, and I struggle to hold them in while I frantically try to remember a spell—any spell—to control them.

Two spells from the spell books I've absorbed shoot to the surface, both used to direct magic, one for each type. Each has a specific rune, and they rise from under my skin and appear on my forearms.

The animal magic rune is on one forearm, an intersecting pattern of hard lines. The earth magic rune is on the other, its design more curved. The effect on both sides of my magic is immediate. The runes focus both of them, taming them so I can direct and manage how the magic is used.

My heart speeds up. My magic is no longer tangled and chaotic. I can feel the strands flowing out from me, smooth and clear.

For the first time, I can control my magic. I can use it. The feeling is euphoric.

This changes *everything*.

The animal magic spell is for bending flesh, and I direct it toward the Unseen, envisioning his bones breaking and his body wrenching itself apart. The earth magic spell I aim at the stone beneath his feet, concentrating on softening the paving. It'll pull him through the floor, trapping him inside.

A rush of triumph fills me as the magic—directed through the runes—obeys my commands, the full force of both types of energy slamming into the places I direct it.

The Unseen's face wavers and distorts, the bending spell already working even as the stone floor beneath him sucks him downward.

This is it. My magic is finally working as it should. I'm so euphoric, I feel like I'm glowing.

But the glowing isn't coming from me.

The Unseen's skin gleams with a cold red light that cuts through the gloom of the basement. He lifts his hands and pulls the strands of my magic away from where I was directing it, dragging it into himself. The untangled strands I was so proud of are sucked effortlessly into his own body.

He's absorbing my magic.

The glow fades and the Unseen smiles, displaying his rotten pointed teeth. His body is the same as it's always been, and his feet are firmly placed on the solid stone floor.

I feel like I'm going to be sick.

"Nice try." He smirks. "My dark magic is far more powerful than yours will ever be."

Then he throws out his hands, and a blast of air hits me square on the chest. It throws me backward and I slam into one of his giant bookcases before hitting the floor. Pain lights up my body, and I struggle to breathe. Above me, the bookcase creaks and sways. Almost in slow motion, the heavy piece of furniture tips, and starts to fall. Books rain down on me.

With the last scraps of power I have remaining, I reach inside me and pull two more runes to the surface of my skin. They're fast and desperate, the first ones I can grab. The animal magic arcs toward the Unseen, and I feel him sucking it in, as though he's feeding on it.

But it's the earth magic I need now. It softens the stone floor beneath me, so when the bookcase slams down, it pushes me into the stone floor as though I'm lying on sponge.

As soon as the bookcase lands, I realize I've trapped myself.

I'm lying in a stone coffin, with the bookcase as the lid, covered in dark magic grimoires. My gasping breaths are all I can hear, and the only light comes from the red glow of my mother's ring.

The weight of the bookcase pushes the grimoires into my flesh. Their dark magic is slimy and dirty and makes my skin crawl.

But on the bright side, at least I'm not as dead as I should be.

"Did you kill her?" Xander's voice is muffled.

"Perhaps. But now that I have her blood and I've absorbed most of her magic, I don't need her to complete the spell. I'll sacrifice the other one, and her death will give us enough power."

"Then get on with it. Start the ceremony."

Jess lets out a moan of pain. "Don't," she chokes out. "Stop."

I struggle, trying to push my way out from under the bookcase. If I don't do something quickly, they'll kill her. But my magic is depleted, and the giant bookcase won't budge, even when I shove it with all my strength. It's too heavy to move.

I'm trapped.

Sagging, I let my hands drop. What am I going to do if I get out of here anyway? The Unseen's dark magic is far too strong for me. I need something more, another way to beat him. Another way to save Xander and Jess. My breath hitches and I have to consciously calm myself down, force myself to think.

It's difficult to stay composed. The grimoires on top of me are trembling with so much power, it sets my teeth on edge. They're written in blood, imbued with the power of the dark witches who created them. I slam my fist into one of the books, my frustration boiling over. Much good it does. The book lets off a little spark of magic after I hit it, drinking in my pain.

As repulsed as I am by the dark magic that's inside the grimoires, a small voice in the corner of my mind whispers seductively to me. The spells inside these books could help me. They'd make me powerful enough to overcome the Unseen and save Jess and Xander. It would be easy. All I'd have to do is—

I let out a strangled curse.

I can't use dark magic. I can't even let myself consider it.

From outside my prison, Jess screams, and the sound is so full of pain it rips my heart into pieces. I can't lie here and do nothing. I have to save her.

My arms have dark magic grimoires open on top of them, and the pages of one are pressing against the back of my hand. My hand is still coated with blood from where the Unseen cut it. All I need to do is turn my hand over and press my bloody palm against the page, let the book absorb some of my magic, and then…

I screw my eyes shut.

I can't do it. Using dark magic will turn me into a monster, just like the Unseen. Aunt Therese knew him, maybe even loved him, and now he's working with

Jeqabeel to destroy the world. He sharpens his teeth, for crying out loud.

That's what'll happen to me if I give in.

Jess screams again, and the sound is a physical pain that stabs through me.

Absorbing the grimoires' dark magic would change me, but what will I become if I let my best friend die without doing everything I can to help her? What kind of monster would *that* make me?

With my stomach churning, and the absolute certainty that this is the worst possible thing I could do, I turn my hand over and let my blood seep into the dark magic grimoire. The *Binde Magick* rune rises to the surface, soaked with my blood, mingling with the blood of the spells written on the pages of the grimoire.

There's no coming back from this. Once the dark magic is inside me, it'll drive me mad.

My hand sinks into the book. Pain burns up my arm, and with it a deathly cold chill that seeps all the way into my bones. My skin prickles and I feel the blood-soaked words slithering their way out of the grimoire.

Then all its dark, blood-infused spells pour into me.

Chapter Twenty-Two

At first, the grimoire's magic feels dirty, like I'm swallowing something slimy, wriggling, and nasty. I feel like throwing up, or turning my own skin inside out just to get rid of it. But as it builds, the energy turns into a hot rush of power that spreads through my limbs, making me tingle all over. This power is like nothing I've ever experienced before.

The pain in my arm turns to pure pleasure.

I gasp, closing my eyes to savor the way it feels. The spells dance and writhe over my skin. The blood of the dark witch who wrote the grimoire is interweaving with my magic, and I have to stop myself from moaning out loud.

Of all the spells in the book, I'll only be able to use the ones that work with animal and earth magic. But even if the others stay inactive, the power I've absorbed with them is making me strong.

Should I absorb the spells from another grimoire? I already feel like I could take on the Unseen with the power I've just ingested. But I've gone this far…there's no point stopping now.

Quickly, I press my hand against the pages of another book, absorbing more dark magic spells. Line by line, letter by letter they crawl up my arm, filling me with their power.

But this is too slow. I need to absorb more books at one time.

The stone floor has hardened around me, my shape permanently imprinted in the rock. By dragging my arms against the rough surface, I graze my skin, bringing up more pinpricks of blood. And pinpricks are all I need.

My blood seeps into more books, and I suck up their spells hungrily. The *Binde Magick* rune feels like it's burning a hole in my hand, but I don't care. The power I'm absorbing is too intoxicating to stop now. I want is to gorge myself, to lap up every last glorious drop.

Then Jess whimpers, and as quickly as it arrived, my euphoria dies.

I forgot about Jess.

The ease with which I was distracted sends a chill through me. I'm not in control of myself. I haven't even used it, and the dark magic is changing me.

I clench my fists over the cuts on my palms. No more.

To be able to use the dark magic, I'd need to take someone else's blood, and I'm not sure I can do that. But at least my earth and animal magic feel replenished. The dark magic seethes below them, like a bomb with no fuse. I can't set it off, but it's strengthened my own magic.

Outside my prison, Jess makes another strangled noise. Not a scream, more like the noise you make when you can no longer scream. I let out a long breath, then use one of the original runes I absorbed from Arabella Lightfoot's book to focus my earth magic and make the stone floor rise on one side. It swells like a wave, and the bookcase slides off, releasing me from my stone coffin.

When I stand up, Xander is in front of the spell-casting

table. He's taken off his shirt, and the Unseen is carving a large, complicated rune into his chest with a blood-covered knife.

The Unseen ignores me, but Xander turns. "You couldn't bear to miss my transformation?" he drawls. "How sweet. You're just in time."

He's so obviously unconcerned by what I just did, it sends a cold shiver of uncertainty into the pit of my stomach. Even with the dark magic thrumming inside me, the demon is stronger than I am.

There are two grimoires open on the table. Glowing on the pages of one of them is the rune the Unseen is carving. It's a complex design and he's copying it exactly. On the open page of the other grimoire, the words of a spell emanate with so much power they shimmer like a mirage. Those spells must be what the Unseen is using to channel enough power into the demon to allow it to break free of Xander's body.

The rune on Xander's chest looks almost complete. The Unseen is carving it so deeply that blood is running down Xander's legs, dripping onto the floor. I don't know if the real Xander can feel pain while the demon is in control of him, but I really hope not.

Jess is on the chair beside the table, also covered in blood. Her head hangs limply, and my heart contracts. Am I too late? Is she already dead?

The Unseen finally straightens, turning away from Xander's bare chest with his knife dripping. "Well, well," he says as if he's only just noticing me. "The bookcase didn't kill you after all."

"Sacrifice them both," Xander orders the Unseen. "The more power I take in, the easier it will be for me to assume my true form. Kill them at the moment of my rebirth."

The Unseen nods. "Of course, my lord."

I take a step forward, my fists clenched. "I won't let you hurt Jess."

"And how exactly do you intend to stop me?" Dropping the knife on the table, the Unseen opens both blood-covered hands and gestures toward one of the bookcases that are still standing, muttering words I can't understand.

The air lights up with a red glow, then a large glass vial flies off the shelf and hits my chest so hard it smashes into pieces, shards of glass crashing to the floor around me.

Liquid sprays out of the vial.

No, not liquid. It's *goo*. A dark, viscous slime is splattered all over me, coating my arms and chest.

"What the—?" I try to lift my hands to wipe it off, but they won't move. The goo is stickier than any glue. It feels soft and like it should be pliable, as though I should be able to yank my hands right back out of it. But they're stuck fast.

Worse, it's covered all the small cuts on my arms and hands, sealing in my blood.

Sealing in my magic.

I take a step, and my boot gets stuck. The goo has dripped down my body onto the ground. I try in vain to peel my foot off the floor, and find the other boot is glued down too.

Gritting my teeth, I try wriggling my fingers, desperate to work them free. My heart is pounding and I want to scream with rage.

"Can't move, Sapphira?" asks the Unseen. "It must be so frustrating for you." He gives me a gloating smile. "Your aunt used to get frustrated with me too. But she never really understood me."

The mention of my Aunt Therese sends a fresh rush of anger through me. I yank my hands, twisting my torso like an escape artist trying to get out of a straitjacket. But for all the good it's doing, I may as well save my strength.

Beside me, Jess is hanging limply off the chair, and I can't tell if she's alive.

How did it come to this?

My best friend is going to be sacrificed. The guy I've fallen for is about to be destroyed.

And I can't do a thing to stop it.

Chapter Twenty-Three

The Unseen picks up the knife from the table, and bends to the rune he's carving on Xander's chest.

Xander doesn't deserve this. All he did was believe in me, trust me.

A stubborn fury boils inside me. It's the same feeling I had when the Blood Council bound my magic and kicked me out of the witch community. I'm going to save him if it's the last thing I do. There must be a way to get the blood my magic needs.

More smoke is pouring from the rune on Xander's chest. This close, its stench is hard to bear. Beside Xander, the demon's body is forming. It towers above him, its jackal-shaped head brushing against the ceiling. Its shoulders are wide and its long arms hang halfway down its thighs. Clawed hands clench and unclench as the dark form solidifies.

"Almost done," mutters the Unseen, carving his design into Xander's flesh. Then he straightens. "There. That's it."

As though a red light has switched on inside Xander,

the complex design carved into his chest bursts forth with a blazing glow. Xander's feet leave the floor. He rises into the air, floating above it. Behind him, the demon's shape is thick and dark.

"Free me from the human. Do it now!" The words come from Xander's mouth in the demon's drawl, his voice deep and rough.

The Unseen stands in front of Xander and lifts the large ceremonial knife above his head, holding it with both hands. My heart speeds up and time seems to slow down, each horrifying moment stretching for a painful eternity. The knife hangs in the air while I strain every muscle as hard as I can, fighting to pull my feet free from my stuck boots, and my arms out of the goo. I have to stop what's about to happen.

But I can't.

The Unseen plunges the knife deep into Xander's torso, sinking the blade into the center of the rune.

Xander screams, but the sound is ecstatic, almost orgasmic. His body lifts higher into the air, his head and arms lolling backward. The knife is buried up to its hilt in Xander's body.

The demon is becoming more solid. Fur is forming. Claws. Its eyes glow red. When it opens its mouth, I catch the glint of fangs. When it speaks again, its voice comes from its own, demonic form.

"Sacrifice them," it roars.

The Unseen yanks the knife out of Xander's chest with an effort, using both hands and grunting as he works it free. Xander hangs suspended in the air for a moment longer, then he collapses to the floor, his body limp and lifeless.

He's dead.

Oh God. Xander is *dead*.

If I thought I was broken before, I'm fragmented into tiny pieces now.

The last dregs of my magic come storming up from deep inside me, fighting to get free. It's not powerful, I've used my magic too many times today for there to be much left. But it's the embodiment of chaos, reacting to the heartbreak that's splintering me apart.

I need fresh blood to let the magic out, but with my hands trapped in goo, I can't cut myself.

"Ratticus," I shout. "Help me! Bite me!"

"*Are you nuts?*" The reply in my head is thin and reedy. "*I'm staying right here.*"

I want to scream.

If I don't manage to draw blood in the next few seconds, the Unseen will kill me too.

Gritting my teeth, I focus all my strength on yanking one finger free of the goo. The index finger on my right hand feels like it's the least stuck, and even if I have to leave my skin behind, I'm going to drag it free.

Gasping, ignoring the pain, I tear it slowly out of the goo. Sure enough, some of my skin peels away, leaving my finger raw.

Spots of blood well up.

My magic rises with it.

I bring up a rune to control my animal magic, holding it in while I let my earth magic out, directing it into the largest piece of stone in the room.

I slam it into the ugly statue in the corner of the room —the eight-legged, horned creature that must have come straight from its creator's nightmares.

The statue moves. But it's not the avenging monster I hoped for.

The eight-legged creature takes a lumbering, ponderous step forward, its multitude of legs moving stiffly, as though in slow motion. It reminds me of a sloth, moving so slowly that it'll never be able to stop anything in time. Like I've summoned a glacier to come to my rescue.

Hissing with frustration, I fight to pull another finger free, to get more blood, but the goo is too strong. I've wasted what was left of my magic on a creeping monolith.

The Unseen turns to look at it. He chuckles, glancing back at me with a small shake of his head. It's moving so slowly, he doesn't even bother to counter my magic. The stone monster takes another step, stone scraping against stone as it drags its feet forward, the sound rumbling like the slowest avalanche in the world. I want to scream at it to move faster, to leap at the Unseen, to do anything other than this excruciating dawdle.

"Would you stop messing around and do something useful?" Ratticus's voice fills my head, but I still can't see the little coward. If he'd shown a bit of bravery and bitten me, the magic might have had more blood to power it.

Stepping closer to me, the Unseen's eyes are dark with anticipation. Behind him, the statue laboriously drags its legs forward once more. I'll be dead of old age before it gets anywhere close enough to help me.

The demon is still solidifying, and the Unseen's bloody knife is clenched in both hands. He's ready to stab me in the heart and finish the demon's resurrection.

As the statue sags, finally running out of what little steam it had, I spot something scuttling up its back. Ratticus must have been hiding behind it, and now he's searching out a new hiding place, his little nose twitching with fear.

My animal magic still pulses inside me. Could this be a way out?

I look down at the rune on my arm that's holding my animal magic contained. It's coated with a layer of goo, but under my gaze, the rune pulses, then transforms. I make it form the shape of a different rune.

Though I still can't move, I can make another creature move for me. The rune is for entering the minds of small animals, and I direct my animal magic toward Ratticus.

Fear floods my brain. My vision is blurred, sounds are distorted, smells are sharp. My thoughts are all of running, hiding, getting out of this basement and away from the demon that smells scarily like a dog. Annoyance at the hopeless witch whose magic isn't helping—me—is overwhelming. Dreams of tasty food and being pampered are also swimming around in there.

I'm in Ratticus's head. I'm seeing what he sees, feeling what he feels.

"Get out! Stop it!"

He's realized I'm inside him. Panic flares, and he tries to run away, down the back of the statue.

But he's too late. I'm controlling him. Overriding his fear, I focus his thoughts on something else. I give him one goal, one desire. One purpose.

Rip open the Unseen's neck.

I wrench my mind from his.

As the Unseen lifts his knife over my chest, the small rat runs across one of the statue's extended legs and launches himself at the Unseen. Ratticus lands on the Unseen's leg and scrambles up his clothes, climbing with his sharp claws.

The Unseen flinches back, trying to shake the small creature off, but the rat is determined. Reaching his shoulder, Ratticus buries his fangs into the Unseen's neck.

The Unseen yelps, swiping at him with the hand not holding the knife. Ratticus clings on, using his teeth and claws to keep himself attached, but the Unseen finally manages to dislodge him, knocking the rat onto his chest.

My intention was for Ratticus to tear open the Unseen's jugular. But there's no gaping wound, no gushing torrent of blood. Instead, I have to squint to make out the tiny cut on the Unseen's neck and a microscopic red trickle.

I may have vastly overestimated the size of Ratticus's tiny fangs.

All the breath escapes my lungs in a despairing rush. That turned out to be as helpful as the statue's slow-motion charge.

But Ratticus is still scrambling over the Unseen's clothes, and as the dark witch tries to dislodge him, he swings around wildly. A few small drops of blood fly off the knife he's holding and spatter onto my arm.

Four tiny drops of Xander's blood.

It's enough.

The dark magic inside me flares into life as it feeds thirstily on the blood. Its power makes me gasp. It fills me with renewed strength, and I feel a surge of fierce joy as I pull two spells from inside me.

My earth magic explodes out of me, fuelled by the dark magic, and focused by one of the runes. It slams into the stone floor at my feet, creating stone hands that rise from the floor like zombie hands rising from a grave. The hands grab the goo and wrench it off my boots, freeing me to step forward.

The other rune directs my animal magic into my own body. My flesh burns as a whole new skin forms on my arms, instantly growing underneath the old one. My old skin peels away, like a snake shedding its skin, taking the goo with it.

The Unseen is still swiping at Ratticus when the rat does a giant leap off him, catapulting himself to safety. With a growl, the Unseen jerks back to me. His eyes glisten with rage, and he slashes at me with the knife. Before the blade can connect with my body, I kick up as hard and as high as I can.

My boot plows into his chest and he falls back into his spell table, knocking it over and sending the grimoires crashing to the floor. The Unseen crumples to the ground. He's probably the most powerful dark witch in existence, but he's also an old man, weak and frail, and the last thing he was expecting was for me to break free from his goo.

He's not moving. Did I knock him out? Is he dead?

I whirl to face the demon. It's still growing, and its hideous form is quickly becoming too big for the Unseen's basement. A body is lying near its feet.

Xander.

He looks lifeless. Except this close, with my dark magic still swirling around me, I realize he's not dead.

Not yet, at least.

Xander's life force is weakening as the last of his blood drains. He's dying fast. I have to stop it, to keep him alive. I glance up at the demon forming in front of me, then at Jess, who's still limply hanging off the chair she's tied to.

I don't know what to do. If I leave Xander, he'll die.

But if I let the demon complete its transformation, we'll all die.

I crouch down and grab Xander's hands, covering my palms with his blood. It may not be the smart thing to do, but I have to try to save him.

As his blood soaks my skin, my dark magic flares again, hot and incredibly strong. The rush of power that fills me feels so good, I can't keep from groaning with pleasure, even as hot tears run down my cheeks. My dark magic is growing even stronger, but Xander's blood isn't enough to sate it. It wants more blood, more pain. I can feel its need, its thirst like an insatiable hole that I'll never be able to fill.

Its thirst is becoming part of me. The realization fills me with sick dread, but I'm too busy summoning a healing spell to worry about it now. As the healing rune appears, I glimpse movement from the corner of my eyes. The Unseen is getting to his feet, swaying unsteadily.

He isn't going to give me enough time to save Xander.

I can see the Unseen's dark magic more clearly now, through the eyes of another practitioner. His power surrounds him, a swirling mass of red tentacles.

He gathers his magic in one hand, and launches a burst of ice at me, sharp pointed shards to rip me apart.

But with my hands in Xander's blood, my own power is burning hot.

I reach inside myself for a spell to deflect his magic, and it's not a rune that comes up, but an incantation. I mutter the words of the spell without having to consciously recall them, as if I've known them forever, and my skin hardens into a tough, rhino-like hide. The ice shards shatter when they hit me, spraying ice fragments everywhere. I don't even feel them.

The Unseen gestures with his hands, as though he's motioning toward his own chest. All the air rushes out of my lungs. My throat closes, so I can't draw a breath. My lungs are empty, crushed flat and my mouth refuses to take in any air.

My dark magic surges again, fuelling my animal magic. A transformation spell. Gills form in my neck, large flaps of skin to let me drag in air. My lungs inflate, the gills opening wide for the air to rush in.

As the dark witch's spell fades, my gills disappear, leaving me gasping and coughing, but alive.

But I'm losing this fight. Instead of defending, I need to attack.

With one hand on Xander, I extend my other hand

toward the Unseen and bring up a rune on my palm. Earth magic, fuelled by the dark magic, bursts forth. The stone floor rumbles and shakes as the earthquake I've created rolls through the room. The Unseen stumbles, grabbing the statue to hold himself steady.

In a quick, reflex move, he draws his arm back and throws his big ceremonial knife.

It whistles toward me.

I stumble back, ducking away, and the knife just misses me. It slams into the wooden bookcase behind me, its blade burying into the spine of a grimoire.

I reach inside me for more magic, searching for a way to end this, but the Unseen's knife throw has driven me away from Xander. His fresh blood was powering my dark magic, and without it, I feel drained. The magic I have left is being fuelled by what little blood remains on my hands. It's no match for the Unseen's power.

The Unseen stumbles toward me, herding me further away from Xander. He's limping badly, as though he wrenched something when he hit the ground. But he's smirking, his lips pulled back from his sharpened teeth in a disgusting smile.

His dark magic seethes and writhes around his body. It grows thicker and thicker, and as he steps even closer, its red tentacles reach for me. They look like eager red snakes, slithering toward me.

"It's been fun, Sapphira. Are you ready to die now?"

Only a few minutes ago, I was swearing I'd never willingly take someone else's blood to power the dark magic. Now, I wish Xander were close enough for me to bend down and flatten my palm against his carved-up chest.

I flinch backward as the Unseen's strands of magic whip out and coil themselves around me. Where they touch my skin, icy cold fingers tear into my flesh, the chill tearing deep into my bones.

My flesh numbs and my legs weaken. I struggle, trying to break free, to get away, but his magic holds me tight and my strength is draining fast. When I lift my hands, they're already shaking.

The Unseen is going to suck the life right out of me.

I can't pull away. His power is too strong.

Reaching deep inside, I drag out the small amount of magic I have left. This is my last chance. It's everything I've got.

As the Unseen's tentacles drag me close, I suck in a deep breath and let my magic loose. At the same moment, I stop struggling and trying to break away. Instead I lunge at him, bringing up one arm while I fling myself forward as hard and as fast as I can.

With my earth magic, I harden my flesh, turning my arm to stone.

With my animal magic, I soften the Unseen's flesh.

My hardened hand meets his chest and sinks into it like jelly. My magic liquefies his ribs as my stone fingers slice into him. My hand is a missile made from rock. I shove through his bones, through muscles, and sinews and tendons. A hole opens in his chest, and I push my hand in deeper as his blood pulses hot and wet around my arm.

His eyes widen in shock, and his grunt expels a gust of hot, foul breath into my face.

His dark magic coils around my arm, already fighting me, pushing me back and trying to close and repair the cavity in his chest. But now his blood and pain are feeding my dark magic, and a hot, overwhelming surge of energy flares through me, helping me force my hand even deeper.

My body is electric. My veins are filled with molten lava, and it feels like I'm finally *alive*. As though I've been living my entire life in a darkened room, and warm light has just flooded in.

I close my eyes, savoring the moment as I open my fingers and grasp the warmth of the Unseen's heart. It beats hard against my toughened palm.

Then I yank it right out of his chest.

"Take that, you ugly bastard!" Jess must have just regained consciousness, and her voice is weak and hoarse, barely more than a whisper. "That's for the all shit you pulled." Her bloodied hair is sticking up in all directions, and her head sags as though she's having trouble keeping it up.

My gaze jerks back to the Unseen as he collapses, his body dropping heavily to the floor at my feet.

His heart pulses in my hand, still beating strongly, as though it doesn't realize it has no more blood to pump, no body left to serve.

For a moment, my dark power rejoices, and I have an overwhelming urge to squeeze the Unseen's still-beating heart, to crush it between my fingers. Then I catch myself. What the hell?

Shivering with revulsion, I let the heart drop.

The Unseen's dark magic seethes and writhes around his dead body. But instead of dissipating as he dies, it's being sucked away.

My breath hitches as I realize where it's going.

Jeqabeel is absorbing the Unseen's power, pulling it into itself. The demon is using the Unseen's death to power its final transformation.

The demon's body is now fully solid. It's standing up like a man, but covered with a hairy pelt and a jackal's head. It lifts its oversized arms to stretch out its enormous claws. Jeqabeel's eyes glow red and its hairy muzzle opens as though it's grinning.

It throws back its head and gives a triumphant laugh. "You're a worthy servant," it roars. "Such a magnificent sacrifice has all but completed my transformation."

My stomach turns itself inside out. "I'm not your servant!"

But when the demon laugh turns scornful, my breath catches.

Could I have been doing what it wanted all along?

By killing the Unseen, I've given the demon the sacrifice it needed. The Unseen's dark magic was stronger than mine, so his death has given the demon a lot more power than if I'd been sacrificed.

I pulled out the Unseen's still-beating heart, just like the demon did to my mother. Like it did to Sylvia and Mireya.

That can't be a coincidence.

"Were you controlling me?" I whisper. Somehow the demon must have influenced me to kill the Unseen that way. It's the only explanation.

The demon's power swirls around me, pressing against me like it's looking for a way in, a way to take everything from me. Its power is oppressive. It fills the Unseen's basement like a dark, pulsing slime.

The demon wants my dark magic, too. It wants my life. And even with the power I've gained from killing the Unseen, there's no way I'm strong enough to stop it.

"You finally did something right," squeaks Ratticus in my head. *"Keep helping the demon, and maybe it'll let us live."*

Chapter Twenty-Four

Jeqabeel's magic wraps tightly around me, pushing so hard I can barely breathe.

"I need more blood," the demon snarls. "Submit to my will. Gather blood for me and live."

I shake my head, unable to respond any other way. I still can't believe what I just did.

The demon's magic tightens, squeezing my chest and pressing against my face. I want to cough, but I don't have enough air. My mouth opens and I suck the demon's dark energy down my throat.

"Here's a taste of the magic my servants command."

Power fills me, far greater than the surge of dark magic I felt when I killed the Unseen. This rush is so intense that if the demon's power weren't holding me upright, I'd sink to my knees. It electrifies every cell in my body.

With that power, I could do and have anything I wanted.

I could bring the dead to life. Not just Xander, Sylvia, and Aunt Therese. I could have my parents back. The thought makes my heart ache with unbearable longing.

For a moment I hold the entire world in the palm of one hand, revelling in the knowledge that I could shape it exactly the way I want.

Then the demon withdraws its magic and I drop to the ground, gasping with shock and loss. To be given that much power for just a moment, and then have it taken away, is almost enough to drive me insane. It's so much worse than never getting to glimpse it at all.

Now I know why Uncle Ray and the Unseen wanted to release Jeqabeel. For the first time, I completely understand. Nothing I've ever felt comes anywhere close to what the demon offers.

I drop my head, my chest heaving. My yearning for the demon's power is so strong, it almost overrides everything.

Almost.

Because what the demon really wants is to use me. It wants the dark power I absorbed from the grimoires, my animal and earth magic, and any remaining power from my Blood Council bond. Once it's taken my magic, it'll spit out my corpse. Then it'll do the same to every living thing on the planet. It has no morals, no conscience. It'll wipe everything out. And I'm the only person with any chance of stopping it.

Still, I have to curl my hands into fists to fight the almost uncontrollable urge to give in to the demon and take the power it's offering. My body shakes and I feel like I'm being torn apart from the inside.

"I need more blood," roars Jeqabeel. "I need more power." It lifts its clawed hands and something weird happens. For just an instant, its solid form doesn't seem quite so solid. Like for a moment it wavered.

"Kill the witch," it demands, pointing at Jess. "Do it now."

Jess lifts her face. She blinks as though her vision is

fuzzy, then fixes her bloodshot eyes on the demon. It towers over us both, its stench almost as overwhelming as its size. Its clawed hands look huge enough to kill us with one swipe. But Jess manages to sneer at it like she's not afraid.

It's more than I can do right now. "Jess isn't a witch," I tell the demon. "She has no magic." My stomach clenches at the thought of harming Jess, but the thought of the power I could wield is still seductive. I'm having a hard time thinking about anything else.

The demon snarls. "The witch has strong magic. Kill her so I can feed on her power."

Jess has magic?

Jess blinks at the demon, her expression turning confused. "I don't have magic," she croaks.

But now I can see that the demon's right, there's an aura of power around her. I think the dark magic I absorbed must have enhanced my senses, because I haven't noticed it before, but she's definitely giving off a warm, vibrant energy.

"Kill her," the demon roars.

"I don't have magic." Jess's voice is slurred, and her eyelids slowly lower, like she's losing consciousness again.

I can't tell if she's pretending not to know about her magic, or if she's really clueless. My head hurts, and suddenly I'm having a hard time focusing on what's important. The memory of the demon's power lies too heavily over me, making it hard to think straight. Wouldn't it be easier to give in to the demon, to accept my role as its helper and take what it's offering?

After all, Jess lied to me. She's been lying to me since the first day we met.

I grit my teeth and nod at the demon. "Okay. I'll do it."

Jess's eyes focus on me. "What?" Her slurred voice strengthens. "Did you just say you'll kill me?"

"That's good. Go along with what the demon wants so we can get out of here."

I don't know where Ratticus is hiding, but his reedy voice is loud in my head.

The knife the Unseen threw at me is still poking out of the bookcase, its blade embedded in the spine of a book. I pull it out, testing its weight in my hand.

Jess has been tortured. She's been suffering for hours. The Unseen said her blood was rich with her agony. He was right. I can sense it. The dark magic's need for blood burns inside me, and that need has been heightened by the power Jeqabeel allowed me to glimpse.

I *want* to take Jess's blood. I want to soak my hands in it and fill myself with dark, glorious energy.

A dark voice whispers inside me.

Jess lied to me.

Jess betrayed me.

Jess deserves to die.

With the knife in my hand, I walk over to Jess. I close my eyes for a moment, gathering my strength. When I open them again, Jess is staring up at me.

"What are you waiting for, Saffy?" she croaks. "Cut the ropes. Get me out of this damn chair."

"I'm sorry." My voice comes out loud and harsh. "I can't do that."

"Saffy, don't be stupid. Just get me out of here!"

I lift the hand holding the knife, and something red glints in the darkness.

My mother's ring.

I hesitate, thinking about what she'd say if she could see me now. How disappointed she'd be. On the other hand, what if I do what the demon wants and it gives me the power to bring my mother back to life? What price would be too much to get her back?

"How about I promise to clean the house more often? And I'll do double the washing up. Just get me the hell loose from here, Saff!" Jess is acting brave, trying to make light of it, but I can see the fear in her eyes.

"You don't understand. I have to do this."

She growls as I loom over her. "Stop it, Saffy. Put the knife down. Think about what you're doing."

"Kill her," snarls the demon. "Do it now."

"*Less talking, more slicing*," agrees Ratticus.

I shut out all their voices, focusing on what I'm about to do. When I put my hand on Jess's blood-smeared arm, her magic calls to me. Even old and dry, her blood tingles my palm with its power.

How much more power will her fresh blood have, especially when it's infused with her pain?

Licking my lips, I set the knife's blade against her bicep. Jess struggles against the ropes that bind her to the chair. "Touch me with that knife and I'm moving out," she snaps.

"I'm sorry," I murmur. In one quick movement, I slice the knife into her flesh.

Jess hisses with pain. My magic flares as blood runs from the wound.

"Yes," gloats the demon. "Cut her. Bleed her. Kill her."

I put my hand over the wound, soaking my fingers in Jess's blood. My mother's ring glows red and my dark magic builds, the feeling so intensely pleasurable that I drag in a shaky breath.

Jess's magic is a type I've never felt before, something entirely new. It's powerful and intoxicating. I can understand why Jeqabeel wants it.

"Cut her again," the demon orders, its voice a satisfied hiss. "I need more."

Jess's magic coils toward the demon. Jeqabeel is going to absorb it, just like it did to the Unseen. It's going to use her power to make its body completely solid. Then it'll be free to do its own killing, and I have no doubt it'll start with me.

"Saffy." The word is little more than a whisper. Jess's expression is full of betrayal. She stares at me with dark eyes, as though seeing me for the first time.

I feel dirty. Like a monster. But this is who I am now—a dark witch who thrives on other people's blood. That was the decision I made when I took the spells from the grimoires.

I reach deep inside me, taking hold of a spell. When it rises, its words crawl over my skin, running painfully along my nerve endings. Its rune glows hot on my palm.

My power glows unbearably hot inside me. I've spilled blood to cast this magic. And not just any blood. The blood of somebody I love.

Dropping the knife, I lift my hand toward the demon. Dark magic explodes out from my palm, focused by the rune and powered by Jess's suffering and blood. My mother's ring hums with power, glowing bright. It helps me channel everything I have.

The dark magic engulfs Jeqabeel.

I wrap the magic tightly around the demon before making the magical strands harden into stone. The strands loop around it again and again, binding it in cords that turn to stone as they tighten and compress, getting smaller as they get harder. Squeezing the demon tightly enough to crush it.

The council wanted to trap the demon inside Xander by turning him into a statue. Now I'm going to do the same thing by entombing the demon in as much rock as I can summon.

The demon tries to struggle, but the strands keep building, whipping around it faster and faster, thicker and thicker, until it's surrounded by layers upon layers of stone. Then I pull stone from the walls of the basement, from the floor. I pile it all over the demon, being careful not to bury Xander as I slam tons of rock onto Jeqabeel.

When my magic is spent, I stare at the stone mountain in front of me. It's so enormous it takes up most of the basement. Xander lies beside it, his lifeless body dwarfed.

Jess gapes at it, her mouth slack. "Holy crap," she whispers.

I nod wordlessly. Have I done it? Have I actually managed to trap the demon?

"*Finally*," squeaks Ratticus. One of the grimoires scattered around the fallen bookcase shifts, and his twitching nose pokes out from under it. "*Now that you're done screwing around, how about you get me out of here?*"

My gaze drops to Xander, and I crouch beside him, my heart thudding. Maybe he's not dead. Perhaps I can—

An explosion of air slams me back against the wall. My head spinning, I stare at the demon's enormous black form. The rock mountain is gone. Vaporized, as though it never existed.

Jeqabeel throws back its head and roars, baring its long jackal's fangs.

Ratticus squeaks and ducks back under the grimoire. "*Great job, genius. Now you've made it angry.*"

A black pit of despair opens up inside my stomach.

I failed.

I injured Jess to cast that spell, and couldn't trap the demon for longer than a few seconds. Its power still seethes around it, strong enough to make it difficult to pull air into my lungs.

The demon sweeps one of its long arms and its magic

hits me like a hammer, slamming me to the ground. I land hard, the wind knocked out of me. Jess falls too, knocked over in her chair to land on the hard floor. Her head smacks against the stone with a cracking sound that makes me feel sick.

Beside Xander are the two dark magic grimoires that toppled from the Unseen's overturned spell casting table. Their pages shimmer with an oppressive energy that feels more sinister than any of the other grimoires I absorbed. Still, I scramble over and sink my hands into them, drawing their spells inside me.

These spells feel icy cold. They claw and scratch their way inside me, every word as sharp as a dagger. They're the spells the Unseen used to give the demon its physical form.

The dark, nasty spells slice into my body, forcing themselves into every cell, becoming as much a part of me as my muscles and sinews.

If only those spells had never existed, then Jeqabeel would never have managed to create his physical—

Wait.

Can I use these spells to pull that magic back out of the demon?

Can I reverse what the Unseen did? Just like I reversed the spells on Agnes, the gargoyle, and Ratticus?

I reach inside me for the same rune that the Unseen carved into Xander's chest.

Bringing it to the surface of my skin I feel it sear into my own chest. The pain builds, the rune carving itself into me, the same way the Unseen carved it into Xander. It hurts so much, it's unbearable. I open my mouth to scream, and can't hear my own agonized sounds over the throbbing in my ears.

Somehow, through the pain, I manage to bring the

words from the other grimoire up so they run over my skin, the spell unravelling as the words sear themselves into my flesh. They hiss and burn, and my skin smokes.

Jeqabeel snarls.

I need more power.

I put my hand on Xander's bloody chest, covering my skin with his blood. Just as I hoped, he's still alive. Barely.

He's in terrible pain as his body shuts down. He's lost too much blood to last much longer, and his lungs are fighting to drag in whatever scraps of oxygen they can. His agony makes my dark magic surge. As his lungs burn and his heart shudders, the rush of pure, glorious pleasure that rushes through me is obscene.

My dark power grows as it drinks up his pain and feeds on the last of the life force that ebbs from him.

I keep my hand clamped to his chest as I unwind the spell the Unseen used to free Jeqabeel from Xander. Slowly, forcefully, I pull the power the demon absorbed back out of Jeqabeel. It's difficult. The power doesn't want to leave the demon. I have to yank it with all my strength. But inch by inch, I'm reversing the creation of his physical form.

The demon howls, but the sound reverberates weirdly, as though it's coming from a throat that's flicking in and out of existence. Jeqabeel's jackal-headed form is breaking down, turning back into oily black smoke.

Then the demon makes another sound. Because it's so unexpected, it takes me a moment to realize what's happening. Jeqabeel is *laughing*.

"You've released me." The words are little more than a hiss. "Now I'm free to seek real power."

Its body is no more than thick smoke now. Smoke that moves in the air like oil across water, and still stinks of the demon.

The smoke twists and writhes in an invisible wind, then it disappears up the stairwell, moving in a mass as though it has a clear destination. A clear purpose.

I don't know where Jeqabeel is going or what the demon intends to do next. All I know is that I didn't destroy it. Not by a long shot.

Chapter Twenty-Five

y breath hitches.

My gaze goes to Xander's limp body.

Jess moans and I force myself to look at her, though it makes my stomach churn to see how badly she's injured. Not only did she crack her head hard on the floor, but she's lost a lot of blood and her face is deathly pale.

At least she can moan. That means she's still alive.

Xander isn't so lucky.

I felt him dying and still I used his blood, his life force, for my dark magic. I fed on his pain.

I stole his last moments of life.

A black pit opens in my heart. Did I do the wrong thing, turning the demon down? If I'd accepted its offer, maybe I could have saved Xander.

As potent as the grimoires inside me are, no witch, not even a dark magic practitioner, can bring the dead back to life. Only the demon could have done that.

Xander's lying on his back, blood smeared over his

bare chest, where the rune cuts through his flesh. There's blood on his face and I wipe it away—

Wait.

I can still feel his life force. It's faint, but my dark magic is still responding to his blood.

My lungs empty on one shuddering exhalation. He's not dead. Not yet.

"Xander, stay with me. I'm going to fix this, just please stay with me."

I put my hands on his chest, coating my palms with his blood once more. Then I reach inside me for a healing spell. Problem is, I'm totally exhausted. Spent. Until I recharge, even Xander's blood isn't bringing enough of my magic back to life.

I look over at Jess again. I can see her breathing, and she hasn't lost as much blood as Xander. She'll survive a bit longer without my help.

Xander won't.

A rune appears so faintly on my skin, it looks like a long-faded tattoo.

I focus everything I have inside me at Xander, forcing out every bit of magic. The faint strands that emerge look like mist, they're so weak. But they manage to flow out from me and coat the open wounds on Xander's chest, including the knife wound that brought him to the edge of death.

The magic glows brighter, and then the wounds on his chest start to close, the skin knitting back together as if he was never carved up. Some color comes back to Xander's skin, and I see his chest rise and fall.

Then the healing rune fades completely. I've used up everything I have. There's nothing left.

It's not enough. I can feel how thready Xander's hold

on life is. He might seem better on the outside, but he has internal injuries that need to be healed before he'll be safe.

There's one more thing I can do.

I reach inside me again, and this time I grasp hold of my Blood Council bond. The Unseen used that link to suck magic from the Veritas, Magnus, and Dallas. Though he exhausted it, just like my magic, it slowly refills. Hopefully what little is there will be enough.

Using the Blood Council's magic without their permission isn't exactly going to put me on their Christmas card list. But when I pull their magic out, it sings through my veins. As long as Xander survives, I'll take whatever consequences come my way.

As I pour their energy from my body into his, everything but him seems to shimmer and blur. Xander is the only thing that exists. All I can feel is the connection between us, his deep cuts closing up, and his heart beating more strongly.

Xander opens his eyes. They're light blue, and perfectly clear.

He blinks at me, a slight frown creasing his forehead, and then sucks in a deep breath as if he hasn't done so in a very long time.

"Saffy?" His voice is ragged.

I let out a shuddering sigh and grab hold of his hand with both of mine. "It's me. You're safe now. You're going to be okay."

"What happened?"

I shake my head, unable to stop myself from swaying. I feel so light-headed, I'm afraid I might pass out. I only have a tiny bit of magic left to heal Jess, but I'm worried I might not even be able to get over to where she's lying on the floor, still tied to the chair.

"Your eyes." He blinks at me. "What happened to your eyes?"

"What's wrong with my eyes?" My gaze flickers around the room as if I might find a convenient surface to check them. All I see is dust and blood and destruction.

"They're black. All black." He pulls his hand out of mine and sits up slowly, moving away from me in the process. I don't know if it's on purpose, but I feel the loss of his hand like a piece of me has just been removed.

My heart contracts. The dark magic I used so freely must have changed my eyes. For some reason, the thought that there's physical evidence of my new powers is disconcerting. I don't want people to look at me and know my awful secret.

But I can't worry about it now. Not until I've healed Jess.

"How did we get here?" asks Xander. "Is Jess okay?"

I don't answer immediately, because I'm too busy trying to pull myself back onto my feet. After a couple of failed attempts, I give up and crawl over to Jess's chair.

A grimoire rustles by the fallen bookcase. *"Is it safe to come out?"* asks Ratticus.

Ignoring him, I take a deep breath and drag up every last scrap of magic left inside me. A healing rune appears, a faint haze on my skin. Weak strands of magic flow into her.

The knife wound I gave her disappears, and the burn marks fade to a dull red. I can sense the injury she got from hitting her head. It's repairing, the swelling shrinking.

After a few moments, Jess's eyes flutter open and she blinks woozily at me.

"It's okay Jess," I manage. "They're gone."

My vision is starting to fade, but I pick at the knots in the rope that's binding her to the chair.

Jess's eyes clear, and her face contorts. "Get away from me," she snarls.

My stomach turns over at the anger in her voice. "It's okay. I'm trying to free you." The knots in the rope are blood-soaked and swollen and my fingers are too weak to work them loose.

Xander puts his hand on my shoulder. "I'll untie Jess. Why don't you tell us what happened?"

Jess frowns. "It's fuzzy. All I remember is that she cut me. She was helping the demon."

I sag backward, pulling away from Jess so I don't have to see the anger in her eyes. I deserve her hate. I cut into her and used her blood and suffering. And I felt the power in her blood. Her amazing, electrifying power.

The worst part? Even now, part of me wants more.

"I'm sure she cut you for a reason." Xander sounds calm, working the knots around Jess's wrists undone. "What happened, Saff?"

"She's right." My voice trembles with exhaustion. "I used Jess's blood. I cut her arm and used her blood to cast a spell."

"Dark magic." Jess grimaces with distaste.

I nod. "Dark magic," I repeat in a whisper.

"But did she use it to save us?" He nods in the direction of the Unseen's body lying crumpled on the floor. From this angle the hole in his chest isn't visible, so at least they can't see what I did to him.

Jess pulls one hand free of the rope. "Maybe. But using dark magic makes her as bad as the Unseen."

She's right. The magic inside me is thirsty for blood, and eventually that thirst is going to drive me mad. I wonder how long it was before the Unseen decided filing his teeth into points was a good style option? Years? Months? Days?

"I don't think that's true, and neither do you, Jess." Xander sounds calm. "The last thing I remember is leaving Sylvia's house. I can't hear the demon, so I guess it's out of my head. Please tell me it's dead?" He gives me a hopeful look.

I shake my head.

"Well, at least I'm not its vessel anymore." He offers me a smile before going back to unwinding the rope that holds Jess to the chair.

I'm grateful for that too. Xander looks strong again, and his eyes are ice blue. Seeing him like this reminds me why I absorbed the dark magic.

For the people I love.

I prop myself against the wall and sigh. "The demon escaped. I don't know where it went."

"Then what are you sitting around for?" demands Ratticus. *"Get me out of here."*

"What happened after the Veritas came to Sylvia's house?" asks Xander as he gets the final knot undone, and Jess pulls herself to her feet. His detective's brain is still clearly trying to piece everything together.

I drag a breath. I'm so exhausted, it's hard to get words out. All I want to do is curl up into a ball and pass out. "The council tried to turn you into a statue. The Unseen kidnapped us. The demon was almost resurrected into his physical form."

"How did you kill the Unseen?" asks Xander.

"Are you going to jibber jabber all day?" Ratticus sounds annoyed. *"How about doing less talking and more walking?"*

My thoughts are too confused. I can't think straight, especially not with a rat complaining in my head.

"She looks like she's about to faint." Jess is rubbing the rope marks on her wrists. I wish I had enough magic left to heal them for her.

"The Veritas is probably on her way, with Dallas and Magnus," I murmur. "I need to leave before they arrive." I try to pull myself to my feet, but my legs are too weak and I collapse back on the floor.

"The council will turn you to stone." Jess's expression is grim.

I nod wearily. "I'd rather not let that happen."

"Why would they do that?" demands Xander. "Because you used dark magic to cast a spell that got the demon out of me?"

It's not exactly what happened, but I'm too exhausted to explain, so I just nod, thankful beyond words to be able to gaze into his clear blue eyes instead of the demon's red ones.

He frowns. "Correct me if I'm wrong, but didn't you just save the world? I mean, shouldn't they give you the witch equivalent of a medal? A golden broomstick, or something? You sure as hell deserve it."

Jess is wiping the blood off her face with a corner of her shirt. "They won't see it that way."

I sigh in agreement. My eyes want to close. Keeping them open is taking all my energy.

I hear Xander crossing over to me. Then he drops down next to me and pulls me into his arms, hugging me close. "Come on, we need to get out of here." He smiles down at me. "We're used to being on the run, right?"

"Let's go," I slur. My tongue feels too thick to form words.

I nestle into Xander's arms. To feel his warm body wrapped around me is better than the softest pillow. Better than anything I can imagine.

"*You're not leaving me behind.*" I feel sharp claws on my leg. A small, blood-covered creature scurries up my body and pushes himself into the hair at the nape of my neck.

"What the hell—?" Xander jerks away to stare at the rat on my shoulder. "Is that Ratticus? You found him and turned him back into a normal-sized rat?"

"Has a new name." My words must be almost too slurred for Xander to understand. "I'm going to call him Cowardus."

Ratticus nips my skin with his sharp little teeth. *"Don't be rude, black eyes."*

I want to tell Jess and Xander how sorry I am for everything, but I don't have the strength. The world is slipping away. I'm going to pass out, and while I'm asleep, the council will come and turn me into a statue. I don't have the energy to stop them, and perhaps I shouldn't try.

Dark magic is forbidden for good reason. I don't want to become like the Unseen.

The scary thing? As exhausted as I am, I suspect that if I were to pick up the Unseen's knife and slice somebody open, my exhaustion would fade and my power would return.

I can't pretend part of me isn't tempted.

Chapter Twenty-Six

Xander has his arms around me. "No," he says flatly. "I won't let you take her."

"I'll give you a minute to say goodbye." Magnus sounds gruff. "That's the best I can do."

He walks a short distance away and folds his hands in front of him, looking away, down the street. Behind us is the Unseen's house, a place I'd gladly burn down.

Magnus summoned a witch to take Jess to have her wounds healed, and Xander should have gone too, except he refused to leave me. His stubborn refusal made me feel warm inside, despite the situation.

I'm still weak and exhausted. I'm recovering slowly, but if Xander weren't holding me up, I'd probably keel over. At least my eyes aren't completely black anymore.

"What do they want from you?" demands Xander. "Will they turn you into a statue? They'll have to go through me."

I sigh, wishing Xander and I could go home and curl up in bed. Now he's finally rid of the demon, I'd get to touch him all I want if the council would just leave us be. Why can I never catch a break?

"Unfortunately, I have to go with him," I say reluctantly. "Neither of us can stop the council. They're too strong." I'm not sure that's entirely true, anymore. The dark magic grimoires I absorbed were so powerful, maybe I could walk away from the council and whatever punishment they have planned. But to do that, I'd need to take somebody else's blood.

And as much as the dark magic inside me thirsts for it, I'm not doing it again.

"It'll be fine," I lie.

Xander rests his chin against my forehead. "I'm not going to let you go, so they'll have to take me too."

In spite of knowing my life's on the line, I manage to give Xander a little smile. "Thank you," I whisper. "And I'm sorry about all of this. You only got dragged into it all because of me."

He kisses me softly, and his lips feel so good it makes me want to cling to him.

"It was all worth it if I get to be with you." He grimaces. "Well, to be honest, I could have done without having the demon in my head. And I'm really glad I can't remember having my chest carved up and being stabbed to death. And now I'm kissing a girl who has a rat on her shoulder, so there's that." He grimaces at Ratticus. "But apart from those things, totally worth it."

"What does demon-dude have against rats?" demands an offended-sounding voice in my head.

"You levitated," I tell him, ignoring Ratticus. "It was pretty badass."

"Don't suppose you managed to get a photo? It'd blow up my Instagram."

Magnus clears his throat, and I shoot him a glare.

"He's going to take me soon." I swallow down the lump that's forming in my throat. I can't fall apart in front of Xander. If I do, he'll know Jess wasn't exaggerating about what the council have planned.

But trying to fight it here would put Xander in the firing line. I'll go quietly and pretend everything's fine. And maybe it will be. There's a chance I can convince the council not to turn me into stone. After all, Xander's right, I did save them all.

"You'll be back soon, won't you?" Xander kisses my forehead. "You want me to take Ratticus? I can meet you at your place later?"

There's a very good chance I won't ever get to see my house, or him, again. I should probably tell him the truth, but that would make this far too hard. "I'd love that," I say, without a word of a lie. "Here." I take Ratticus off my shoulder and pass him over to Xander. "Look after the little guy for me, okay?"

"Tell demon-dude I'm hungry," grumbles Ratticus.

"Sapphira, it's time to go." Magnus cuts his hand and draws a rune with the blood, a process that now seems clumsy and slow. I feel Magnus's spell settle over me as he's casting it, and for a moment, I'm filled with an overpowering urge to take Xander's blood and break the spell before it can bind me. His spell is designed to draw me to the council chambers, so I can't try to run. But it's weak. Laughably weak, in fact. Like me, Magnus is probably suffering from having his magic depleted through the council bond.

Instead of fighting it, I untangle myself from Xander's embrace and step away from him. His expression just about kills me, and I turn away quickly so he can't see my regret.

* * *

LAST TIME I was in the council chambers, the Unseen blew the door into a million pieces, and destroyed part of the wall. Since then the room and the door have both been repaired, as good as new.

The benefits of having magic.

When Magnus and I trudge inside, Dallas and the Veritas are already there. The sunlight fills the room from the skylights high above us. Only three members of the council remain. Well, four, if you count me. Not that I'll be a council member for much longer.

At the rate their members keep dying, they might have trouble trying to recruit anyone new to make up their numbers.

Magnus moves to stand in his circle, and folds his hands in front of him. "Sapphira Black," he intones. "You're charged with using dark magic. How do you plead?"

"I only used dark magic to kill the Unseen, who you should have done something about years ago. And then to try to contain the demon. I did what I had to do." I look around at the councillors, trying to find a friendly face.

Dallas is smirking, of course. This is a dream come true for him. He still blames me for his wife's death, and he'd love to see me suffer.

The Veritas's expression is as impassive as ever. Doesn't she care that my life is hanging in the balance?

"You drew on the blood and suffering of others," says Magnus. "You killed a witch and used his death to power your magic."

"Seriously? You're going to complain about me killing the Unseen?"

"We're simply trying to determine what happened,"

says Magnus a little huffily.

"The truth is that the Unseen was a dark witch who was trying to destroy the world," I snap. "How come it's okay for you to let him run around helping demons, but you're punishing me for stopping him?" I'd meant to keep my temper during this hearing, to reason with the council. But my outrage is rising, and my voice is getting louder.

"Not to mention that you planted your daughter in my house to spy on me. And what about the fact that she had no idea she has magic? Want to talk about that, Magnus?"

He glances at his shoes, an uncomfortable expression crossing his face. "That's not what we're here to discuss."

"You just want to find me guilty and get on with your lives as if I didn't just save your asses?"

"We need to know what happened to the demon."

I shake my head. "All I know is that it's not dead. It disappeared, but it'll be back."

Magnus looks at the Veritas. "Have you recovered enough to do the spell?"

The young girl nods, her expression tense.

"Let's get on with it," growls Dallas.

"What spell?' I ask. But they're already drawing blood.

The Veritas's eyes turn completely white, and I feel the council magic inside me unfurl as she draws on it.

The room darkens while her eyes get brighter and brighter. I can't look away from them. Her eyes grow until they dominate her face. They're all I can see.

White fills my vision completely. And then, inside that white, a picture starts to form.

I'm in the Unseen's basement. Xander and the Unseen are both lifeless on the floor, and Jess is tied to the chair. I can smell acrid smoke, and the stench of the demon.

Jeqabeel laughs. "You've released me." Its words hiss once more in my ears.

The demon's body is made up of nothing but oily smoke now, and it's disappearing up the stairwell.

My body dissolves and becomes smoke too. This time, instead of watching the demon vanish, I drift up the stairs after it. The demon slips out of the Unseen's house through an open window. But instead of following the smoke, the vision flickers and changes. I'm not in the Unseen's house anymore. I'm outside, in Federal Hill Park, looking at Baltimore. Or rather, I'm looking at where Baltimore used to be.

My heart clenches.

The city is burning. Buildings have been levelled. Black smoke billows from the flames, darkening the sky and turning day into night. Even from my viewing point, the smoke is thick enough to burn my throat.

In the center of the devastation, I can feel a terrible presence.

Jeqabeel.

The demon has destroyed Baltimore. It's killed thousands of people, and that's just the start. The more lives it takes, the more suffering it causes, the stronger it grows. Thousands more will soon die. More cities will fall.

I try and draw a breath, but I can't. My lungs won't work. The horror of what I'm witnessing has emptied me. I thought I'd saved us. I actually believed I'd made things better.

The scene in front of me wavers, and my vision fills with a pure white light.

Then I'm back in the council chambers, standing in front of the Vertias. Her face is deathly pale and her hands are shaking. "My God," she whispers.

"What was that?" Magnus turns on the Veritas, his eyes wide with shock. "You were supposed to track the demon and discover where its essence has gone."

"I couldn't." Her little-girl lisp somehow makes what we just witnessed even worse. "Sometimes I can't control the visions. You know that."

"That was the future?" asks Dallas. Of the three of them, he looks the least shaken.

The Veritas nods. "Baltimore will burn. It'll happen soon. Within days or weeks."

"Can we can stop it?" asks Magnus.

She lets out a long breath. "Unlikely. But perhaps."

I swallow hard, trying to find my own voice. It's difficult, because my throat still feels raw. "We have to do everything we can to keep that from happening."

Magnus frowns at me. "I'm afraid you won't be part of it, Sapphira. For the crime of using others' blood to cast your dark magic, you must be punished."

"But… no! You're going to need my help to stop the demon from destroying the city." I take a step toward him, clenching my fists. "You can't make me into one of those statues. Not now we know the demon is even stronger than it was."

"Every witch knows the punishment for using dark magic," snarls Dallas.

Magnus nods, his brow pulled down and his eyes haunted. "Now, more than ever, we can't allow evil to take root amongst our kind. I'm sorry, Sapphira. I have no choice."

"No!" I take a step away from them, but the Veritas catches me with her gaze and I'm caught in her eyes again, unable to move or look away.

My breathing shudders as I fight to break free. I can't.

They're going to turn me into a living statue, and then the city will burn.

* * *

Afterword

Dear Wonderful Reader,

Thank you for reading *The Problem With Witches*!

We're so happy you're sharing this adventure with us, because things are starting to get scary. And our questions are building!

Where is the demon hiding, and what is it planning?

How's Saffy going to deal with the demon if the council turn her into a statue?

And will Saffy ever get to enjoy a date night with Xander?

All these burning questions will be answered in *The Danger With Demons*, the third book in the Elemental Witch Series.

Trudi and Tania. x

P.S. You can pick up *The Danger With Demons* from Amazon now.